A _____

CANDLELIGHT TUDOR SPECIAL

CANDLELIGHT REGENCIES

Midnight Surrender

〰〰〰〰〰〰〰〰〰〰〰〰〰〰

Margaret Major Cleaves

A CANDLELIGHT TUDOR SPECIAL

To Ted

Published by
Dell Publishing Co., Inc.
1 Dag Hammarskjold Plaza
New York, New York 10017

Dell ® TM 681510, Dell Publishing Co., Inc.

ISBN: 0-440-15023-X

Printed in the United States of America
First printing—September 1980

Midnight Surrender

Chapter 1

The night was wild, and the cold rain fell in such torrents that Katherine Cranston could scarcely see the path before her. The sky blazed suddenly—a brilliant cobweb of lightning—and Gillyflower reared. Frantically clutching the reins, Katherine leaned forward and yelled words of comfort into her mare's ears. Reassured, the horse once more put all four hooves upon the earth, but in spite of her mistress's urgings, refused to take another step. The moon, breaking through its cover of clouds, illuminated the world beneath it, and Katherine saw that the trail she was following was not passable. A recent rockslide had destroyed the face of the cliff. Now the pathway crumbled into frightening nothingness. Beneath, the sea boiled.

"Good girl, Gilly. Good girl," Katherine murmured, and edged her mount away from the precipice.

Katherine barely felt the water that had soaked through her woolen cap and shirt and was trickling down her neck like icy fingers. The cold wind whipped her cloak, and again the horse reared.

"Steady, Gilly. Steady . . ."

If only she could see The Queen's Light, she could

get her bearings. She could spend the night in the tower and be on her way to Blake's at dawn.

The Queen's Light—so named because her father, Sir Cranston, had erected a stone tower that housed a lamp to warn ships away from the particularly vicious reef that sliced the waters one hundred yards out to sea. Sir Cranston himself was sometimes called The Queen's Light by the locals of the countryside. He had assumed the responsibility of always keeping the lamp burning, especially on nights such as this one, when unlucky ships might be tossed too close to the shore. But tonight for some reason the lamp had gone out, and Katherine knew that she was lost.

Oh, why had she chosen tonight of all nights to run away? She had been impetuous and foolhardy after her terrible argument with her father. Her father would say she was immature and spoiled, that she had run away because he had crossed her for the first time in her life. But he wouldn't say anything until tomorrow morning when he discovered she was missing. By then she and Blake would be together, far, far away. Or would they?

She thought uneasily of Blake—his soft hair curling against his face, his gentle gaze. She remembered too his extreme fear of her father. Behind his back, her father called Blake a puppy, a coward, and still worse names. Would she convince Blake to run away with her? Did he love her more than he feared Sir Cranston?

The wind moaned, and Katherine forgot Blake and her doubts about him. Suddenly, as she urged her horse away from the cliffs and in the direction of the moors, she was desperately afraid. She thought longingly of the warmth and comfort of her thickly curtained bed. But she couldn't go back. Remembering anew her father's terrible anger, she prodded Gillyflower toward the stretch of desolate moorland that she thought lay between herself and the tower. She had always been afraid of the moors. Even in the middle of the day they were eerie. Ages ago ancient men had tormented the earth with their molelike diggings, and now the mines that riddled the moors lay deserted. At least that was what wise folks said. But Katherine was Cornish and therefore superstitious. She had grown up on horror tales of knackers, the ghosts of those dead men, who haunted the mines. Oh, she had been a fool to ride out tonight of all nights and so near the mines.

Dark billowing clouds low on the horizon scuttled across the sky, and the sky again blazed—a crazy patchwork of brilliance streaking inky black—and she saw men close by, two ruffians clothed in soaking rags struggling to heave hogsheads into a rickety wagon. Knackers! Katherine heard her own voice mingle with the roll of thunder as one of the men lunged forward, grabbing the reins of her horse, and the other seized her waist, dragging her to the ground. Her cap fell into the mud and her auburn curls tumbled to her shoulders.

"Why she be a lass—and a pretty one." The speaker's eyes leered.

"A plaything for the two of us when our work be done," the other said.

One of the men placed his boot in the pit of her stomach and pressed her down into the rocks until they cut her flesh. For a moment she was too stunned to react. Then she struggled. The man ground the heel of his boot deeper into her stomach. She screamed with pain. The other man gripped her shoulders. They laughed at her helplessness.

Suddenly she was afraid as she'd never been afraid before. She was alone on the moors with these two men who could do whatever they wanted with her. No one from the castle even knew she was gone. No one could help her. Her mouth went dry, and her lips formed words that made no sound. At last she heard her voice, and it sounded like a stranger's, screaming shakily.

"No! No! Take your hands off me!"

"Not 'til we be done with you, lass." The man who spoke was still laughing.

Katherine screamed again and again, until one of the men clamped a filthy hand to her lips. The other man was pulling her hands behind her back and wrapping them tightly with something coarse that cut into her flesh. She shivered, and their faces blurred strangely. She had never felt so cold. She seemed to be falling endlessly. Then she heard something that had nothing to do with the roar of the wind or the men's crude laughter and jeering voices. Galloping hoofbeats pounded the earth. And a man, a giant dressed all in black, leaped from the back of his stallion with his rapier drawn.

"Off with you, you vagabonds!" No longer laughing, the men hastily abandoned their wagons and scuttled away into the darkness like frightened rats.

Surely she must be dreaming! A lantern was shining in her face, and outlined by its light Katherine saw the strong features of a man staring down at her. He had a long, straight nose, a jutting jaw, and swarthy skin. His eyes were black, as was his hair, and they gleamed harshly as he gazed at her. Had she exchanged one set of captors for another? His hand gently touched her forehead and brushed her hair out of her eyes. Surely her imagination was playing tricks on her. There was no one. She was delirious, dying. The light went out, and for a time she saw and thought no more.

Katherine was vaguely aware of a delicious warmth, of the strange sensation of being wrapped in someone's arms and tightly held. Her brain swirled with the events that had resulted in her misadventure on the moor. Her father's voice was booming, "You shall marry Robert Morley, girl, whether you want to or not, and I'll not discuss it further! You shall marry Robert Morley. You shall marry . . . marry . . . marry . . ."

"Oh, no, Blake, help me. Blake—"

The nightmarish whirl went on and on. She saw herself in a wedding gown standing beside her bridegroom, Robert Morley, the man everyone said had murdered his first wife when he tired of her by pushing her down a flight of stairs. At the altar her bridegroom turned to kiss her. His face was fleshless, his eyes sockets. His skeletal fingers gripped her waist and pushed. She was falling exactly as his first wife had fallen down an endless staircase.

She heard a voice soothing, "There, there my darling, it's only a dream . . ."

* * *

A twig of straw from the mattress scratched Katherine's naked thigh and she stirred, awakening to the gentle patter of rain on thatch and the groaning of a shutter swinging back and forth in the wind. When she opened her eyes, she saw beside her, with his dark head on the same pillow as her own, a man whose face was turned toward hers and whose lips were so near hers it appeared he had fallen asleep just after he'd kissed her good night. The man was a stranger to her, yet for some reason his features were familiar. Her mind cleared, and she remembered suddenly. The moors—the lantern in her face—

She sat up, her mind whirling with questions. Where was she and what was she doing in bed with this man? Had he . . . had they . . . The thought of them together made her grow warm all over, as if she stood too near a fire.

Piled atop a rustic chair in one corner, she saw Richard's clothes—the clothes she had stolen from her cousin to disguise herself as a boy. Had this man removed her clothes himself? She was now wearing an overly large silk shirt with ruffled sleeves, doubtless the property of the man beside her.

She looked down at him and a lock of her hair fell across her eyes. As she brushed back the strand, she was startled. In the early morning light a gold wedding band gleamed faintly on her ring finger.

Again she stared at the man who slept beside her, and new questions formed in her mind. He was certainly very handsome. Sleep softened the line of his jaw and lent a certain gentleness to his full, sensual lips. He no longer looked as fierce as he had on the

14

moors. He moved in his sleep and draped one of his arms across her thighs. At this new familiarity, Katherine jumped as if some wild thing had sneaked beneath the covers and bitten her. She squealed and pushed his arm away, thereby awakening him.

His body tensed instantly, and he awoke, his eyes alert. When he saw her, he relaxed and lay back, drowsily smiling. As he looked at her his smile broadened.

"So you're better at last, after detaining me here in this rude and very uncomfortable cottage for the last thirty-six hours while you ranted and raved. I suppose I should be grateful that at least these peasants have a bed instead of a pallet, and I've had you to share it with me."

"Oh! How . . . how dare you speak to me like that!"

"And I can see by your words and your frown— you really shouldn't frown, it distorts your beauty. And you are very beautiful, every inch of you."

"Oh!" she sputtered, and he placed two large, brown fingers to her lips to silence her. She shrank against the pillow to escape his touch.

"As I was saying, I can see that you are going to be as ungrateful as you have been troublesome. No thanks will I get that I risked my neck to save you from those ruffians, no thanks that I have stayed here and occupied myself with you, when I had other more important matters pressing me."

She glared at him with impotent fury. "I'll . . . I'll not endure your insults a moment longer. I assure you, I am no more anxious for your company than you are for mine." She pushed back the covers, and his gaze drifted lazily to the exposed curve of her legs.

Ignoring his insolent smirk and hastily moving to the edge of the bed, she touched the tips of her toes to the rough-hewn timbers of the floor. Quickly she withdrew them. "Oh . . ." she gasped, shivering. The floor was like ice, as was the damp air of the room. As she struggled to rise, he reached for her. She moved away too quickly and suddenly the room was whirling and blackening with brilliant spots of light piercing the blackness. She lost her footing and toppled.

She was vaguely aware of brown arms swiftly enfolding her and lowering her once more to the bed. He was pulling the covers over them, and she became aware of the delicious warmth of his body next to hers. He was speaking softly, his voice low and resonant, sounding of the west country.

"You're not well enough, my pet, to leave me just now. Do you think I've played nursemaid for almost two days to have you collapse before you've repaid the debt of gratitude you owe me?"

She nodded sleepily, too weary to bristle. He was a difficult man, and it was obvious it delighted him to be so. Still, his embrace afforded warmth and comfort. Never had she felt safer than she did now in his arms. She snuggled closer to him and burrowed her head in the crook of his arm. She was asleep at once.

Chapter 2

A bar of light blazed through the window, and Katherine awoke in bed alone. Wrapping a coarse woolen blanket around her for warmth, she arose from the bed and crossed the room to the window. Beneath, she saw him dressed in the lavish garb of an Elizabethan gentleman. What struck her most was his size. He stood at least six feet four inches tall and his shoulders were massive. He wore a jeweled doublet and bombazine breeches of the finest cloth. A jornet, his cloak, was carelessly thrust back over one shoulder. One of his hands offered Gilly some hay to munch, while the other patted the horse on the neck. He was talking softly to Gilly, and Gilly appeared to be listening with great interest. It was obvious that the man had a way with animals, for Gilly did not normally take to strangers.

Beyond the man and horse, wildflowers bloomed on the moors, blue forget-me-nots mingling with white chervil. Gorse flowered golden everywhere. Above, a sea gull swooped. Suddenly Katherine recognized her surroundings—the loft of Jesse Bodrugan's cottage. Jesse was her father's housekeeper, and there were those who said she was more to him than that.

17

Indeed, she did have the best and the largest cottage on Sir Cranston's estate.

Katherine's heavy copper hair hung loosely about her shoulders, and the man looked up and smiled. There was something in the way he looked at her that excited her. The very air that separated them was charged.

As if wanting to break the spell of that moment, he smiled another jaunty smile, one that was not only insolent but infuriating as well, and called, "Ah, it's good to see you up and on your feet again. I was beginning to think you would sleep the day away."

Remembering all too well how profoundly he had irritated her when she had first come out of her delirium, Katherine's temper flared.

Suddenly she felt dizzy. Groping for a chair, she sank down heavily. The feeling of faintness passed. She heard his tread on the stairs as he took them two at a time.

"Don't come up," she called out. "I'm going to get dressed."

"And what is that to me?" he asked, his head appearing in the doorway. "It was after all I who undressed you. I already know all too well just how charming you are." As he entered the room, her cheeks darkened with embarrassment.

"Sir, would you kindly remove yourself so that I can dress?"

"Anything to oblige a lady—if you still consider yourself one after having spent two nights sleeping with a man who is not your husband."

"Do you mean that we actually, that you . . ."

"That I ravished you while you lay semiconscious

18

beside me? No, I didn't. I won't say the idea didn't occur to me, but I'm not one to abduct and drug a woman so that I can have my way with her. I like my women warm and willing. And I've every hope that you'll be such a woman—"

"Well, I'm not!"

"Perhaps I can teach you things about yourself you haven't yet discovered."

He was grinning, obviously enjoying himself immensely. Suddenly she was furious! Why, he was deliberately baiting her! But she would not give him the satisfaction of seeing her lose her temper. She breathed deeply.

"Kind sir,"—she said the word *kind* as nastily as she knew how—"I would very much appreciate your leaving so that I may dress. I don't feel well." Indeed, she did look pale. "And I'm not up to this banter that seems to amuse you so."

His manner changed abruptly. Something flickered briefly in the depths of his black eyes. Was it concern for her?

"I'll go downstairs and see what I can find to eat," he said. "When you've finished, I'll help you manage the stairs, and you can join me." Then he was gone. She heard his movements, brisk and purposeful, in the room below.

When she descended the stairs, she saw cheeses, Jesse's pastries and cakes, and her flask of wine—everything she'd stolen from the kitchen before running away—spread out like picnic fare upon a crudely fashioned table. The stranger was sitting at the table, and when he saw her, he leapt up and helped her to the table. For a time they ate ravenously and did not talk. She was slicing one of Jesse's cakes when she noticed he had finished eating and was leaning back, his chair cocked on its two back legs while he stared at her. She put the slice of cake down.

"Eat it," he said. "You've had nothing but a little broth these past two days."

She bit off a piece of the cake and chewed slowly, savoring its rich flavor. He watched her eat with satisfaction. And as he sat there, she warmed toward him. After all, she had sorely inconvenienced him, and all that he had done—even removing her wet clothes—he had done for her benefit. She must let his actions count for more than his words.

He was extraordinarily handsome and smiled often, as if relishing every moment that he lived. She realized suddenly that she found his presence stimulating, that she felt more alive with him than she had ever felt before. Every time he looked at her in that boldly appreciative way of his, she felt wonderfully alive.

When she had finished eating, she said, "Thank you for all you've done for me. I'm in your debt."

"It was nothing really, but perhaps we can find a way for you to repay me." He was grinning. "But first, who are you? Where do you live? And what were you doing on the moor?"

"I have questions of my own." She held up her hand, and the wedding band flashed.

"Ah, the ring." Once more he was smiling. "I have learned, from long experience, that when I find a lady whose bed I wish to share, she is much more willing if I offer her such a ring. And no one questions a

20

man who beds his wife." He continued smiling blandly at her as he watched her brow crease.

She managed calmly, "And you always carry such a ring?"

"Always, for just such emergencies." His eyes twinkled.

"You anticipate them, then?"

He laughed aloud. "Are all the Cornish so nosy? My reasons for carrying the ring must remain my secret."

Katherine glared at him, thinking him the worst of scoundrels. His was a perverse charm, but, doubtless, there were those unfortunates who succumbed to it. She imagined it his habit to find women to his liking, woo them with talk of marriage, trick them with a mock wedding ceremony, produce this ring, and thereby seduce them. Oh, he was absolutely horrid!

"Well, I'll not wear your ring a moment longer!" She tugged at it, but could not remove it.

"Allow me." His voice was mocking. He took her hand in his, gently twisted the ring, and removed it. "It is," he said, "a perfect fit. Mayhap at some future time, when your health is better and I've won you over, we may put it to the use I intended it for."

Her cheeks warmed, and she snatched her hand away. He laughed. She was suddenly weary of talking with this man who refused to answer the simplest questions and who so enjoyed embarrassing her.

The thought came to her that it was strange she'd been gone two days and no one had come to look for her. It was strange, also, that the Bodrugans were so long absent from their cottage. What would her father do to her if he found her alone with this stranger? Suppose he were to discover she'd shared this man's bed. She knew she must get away, and quickly.

She placed her hands on the table, and leaning heavily upon them for support, rose. "I have detained you too long already. I thank you for all you've done, but I must be on my way."

"Not so fast!" He was no longer laughing. There was a steely edge to his voice, and one of his large, brown hands wrapped itself tightly around her wrist. "Do you think I've nursed you these two days and nights so that you may run out on me without even telling me who you are, where you live, and what you were doing on the moor?"

"I haven't the time. My father is probably already looking—"

"So you've run away from your father. Why?"

His grip tightened, and she collapsed once more into the chair. "You must tell me, if you want to go." His jaw squared with determination, and Katherine realized her only chance of escape lay in confiding in him, and hoping that he would see things her way.

"I am Katherine Cranston," she began. Did his eyes light with recognition when she said her name? He leaned forward in his chair to listen. "I am the daughter of Sir Cranston, who is the lord of Castle Cranston, the lord of everything and everyone for miles around. The day I left he told me that he had arranged a grand marriage for me to Robert Morley from Plymouth. I pleaded with him, I begged him not to make me marry a stranger, but he is determined. The man's a pirate and a murderer. He killed his first wife by pushing her down a flight of stairs. His own father banished him for ten years. I decided that I wouldn't marry Robert Morley, so I ran away. I stole my cousin Richard's clothes and disguised myself as a boy. I . . . I . . ." she paused.

The stranger's black eyes had softened as she spoke. He had listened to every word of her tale with great interest. For some reason she was glad to confide in him. Even though he was a perfect stranger, he seemed to understand her.

"Katherine, you were a fool to run away alone without a man to protect you. If I hadn't chanced by at just the right moment . . ." His black eyes went wintry. "Don't you ever"—his voice became low but deeply passionate—"ever do something so stupid again! Your disguise would fool no one!" His tone softened. "But you are young and have led a sheltered and, no doubt, a pampered life thus far. What could you know of the world and its evils? I can understand your fear of marrying a stranger, especially one with as unsavory a reputation as Robert Morley's. When one is desperate, one acts desperately."

"You've heard of him, then?"

"And what man from Devon has not? At least he is rich. That is in his favor. And handsome." He was smiling again, as if the subject of Robert Morley afforded him some secret amusement.

"They say he murdered his wife."

"Ah, I'm surprised this tale has followed him here to the very tip of England." His voice was a whisper she could scarcely hear. "Did you know he now stands high in the Queen's favor? If he were as terrible as you say, could he find such honor?" He seemed strangely excited, as if her answer were of great importance to him.

"They say that when a man is young and handsome it is easy to find favor with our Queen," she said.

"She is wise."

"In matters of state, yes. But not always where men are concerned. Remember she favored Robert Dudley who was suspected of poisoning countless people and of killing his first wife, Amy Robsart, by having her pushed down a flight of stairs."

"I can see that when you've made up your mind, there can be no changing it," he said.

Katherine was again aware that time was passing and that her father might find her at any moment.

"Well, I must be going before someone spots Gilly and goes to my father."

Once more his hand gripped her wrist. "But you haven't told me where you are going, or who this infernal Blake is. When you were delirious you called his name with such, shall we say, ardor, that I couldn't help becoming jealous. Is he your lover? Are you running to him?"

Color rushed into her cheeks. "He is not my lover! What do you take me for? He is a neighbor of ours and a dear friend of mine."

"Ah, would that I could become such a dear friend to you, madam," he said sarcastically. He arose and towered over her.

"Oh, you, you're insolent!"

"And were you running to this Blake the night I found you?" His eyes blazed and he spoke harshly. He held both if her hands possessively while staring down at her. She was afraid of him suddenly—too afraid to answer.

"Were you?" He shook her. His eyes still burned with a fierce light.

"Yes. And now that I've told you everything, you must let me go!" She tried to pull away from him, but he held her tightly.

"Now that you've told me everything, I have absolutely no intention of letting you go. It so happens my father is a distant cousin of your father's, and as I have certain business to attend to in Cornwall, your father was kind enough to invite me to stay with him as his guest. There is no way that I, Sir Cranston's kinsman, can let his daughter run away to her lover."

"You must be Stephen San Nicholas, whom we've been expecting this past fortnight."

"None other!"

"Then you're my cousin too! You must help me! You must!"

"No!"

He stared down at her, and his black eyes, intense with passion, glittered coldly. He was very angry, but because she was so angry herself she failed to notice. She only knew he opposed her, just as her father had when he'd told her she must marry Robert Morley whether she wanted to or not. She felt like a spoiled child who, denied her way, was on the verge of throwing a tantrum. She had never felt so filled with hate and fury as she did while glaring up into his unwavering gaze. She wanted to stamp and scream, to pull his hair out, to do anything to make him change his mind. She was tugging and pulling and twisting to escape his grasp, but he was far stronger than she. He crushed her to him, and bent his head over hers.

"Do you think I saved you—to send you to another man when you have yet to repay me the debt of gratitude you owe me?"

Hot words rushed to her lips, but even as she cried out, he was lowering his mouth to hers and kissed her ruthlessly. He released her hands, but still held her to him at her waist and neck. Her rage dissolved and a new and powerful emotion took its place, flooding her with its warmth and making her legs go weak at the knees, so that she clung to him. Involuntarily her lips parted, and she returned his kiss. She stifled the impulse to run her fingers through the darkness of his hair. He was bending her to him, and something in her was yielding.

Her arms circled his narrow waist and she pressed the softness of her body against his lean, hard one. Never had she felt as wonderful as she did now in his arms. His lips traced a tingling path to her throat, and he murmured words of endearment. His hand went beneath the coarse fabric of Richard's shirt and caressed the bare flesh of her back. Suddenly she jumped back, a furious staccato pounding in her throat.

What was the matter with her? Why had she let him kiss her like that? She scarcely knew him! Yet when he held her and kissed her, it seemed as if she'd always known him, as if . . . as if . . . they belonged together.

He watched her face intently, and she feared he found it very easy to read. What would he do if he knew how much she wanted him, if he knew his power over her? She looked away. When he looked at her like that—his black eyes boldly assessing her—she felt as if her heart were melting. Blake had never kissed her like that! Yet this man was little more than a stranger! She was thoroughly confused.

"You see," he said, breaking the spell, "I was right about you. You will be warm and willing and an apt pupil for the lessons I intend to teach you."

It was obvious he felt smug, having proven to her that she could not resist him, that he had hardly to kiss her and she was breathless and flustered. She was enraged that he found her response amusing and that he was joking about it.

"Oh!" She gasped for breath, her passion turning once more to fury. She sprang at him with an incoherent cry, and he dodged. She glared at him, so tall and powerful, so utterly self-possessed, and felt helpless to vent her rage. He was smiling down at her—that lazy, insolent smile that so maddened her. Surely, she had never known such anger! Then his face swirled as did the walls of the cottage and a sickening dizziness swept her. Her knees buckled, and he reached for her and helped her to a chair. "I hate you!" she muttered shakily. "I hate you!"

"Then why are you fainting from my kisses?"

His voice grew dim and his face whirled. She felt sick and heavy. All went black.

When she came to, he was bathing her forehead with a damp rag. His black eyes searched her face anxiously as he reached for the flask of wine and pressed it clumsily to her lips, spilling it down her neck.

"Drink this," he said. She was too tired to resist.

She gulped, choking. "I had forgotten your condition," he said, "or I would never have, shall I say, I would never have forced you to endure my kisses, although I am not sure you were as unwilling as you would have me believe." She was too exhausted to be irritated by his words. "I can see that you're tired," he continued. "We must get you to the castle so you can rest."

The castle and her father and the reality of having to marry Robert Morley loomed before her. Hers had been but a temporary escape.

Chapter 3

The wind was damp and smelled of the sea. Katherine shivered, and Stephen, who was leading the now saddled horses toward her, loosened his own cloak and tossed it to her. "Put it on!" She hesitated. "You act surprised at my gallantry? But you do not know me. I've been at Court where a man who serves the crown must always remember he serves as well a woman, and our Queen is a woman who likes such gallantry. I do not think it wise that I fall out of practice while I stay in Cornwall."

Katherine pulled the cloak over Richard's and tied it. Stephen lifted the hood over her head, and smiled down at her. "Let me help you mount Gilly." His hands circled her waist. "You are very slender," he marveled. "My fingers meet. I've always liked women with tiny waists, especially when they are not so tiny elsewhere." His gaze drifted to the exact spot where his cloak rounded over her bosom.

She flushed, and dared not meet his eyes for fear he would see her confusion. Was it to be like this every time he touched her, every time he made such a remark?

"Stephen! You were helping me to mount!"

"Your beauty distracts me."

"You must try to remember that you are my cousin."

"Only a distant one!"

"My father will not appreciate your flirting with me when he has plans for me to marry someone else."

"Perhaps he will not be as averse to it as you think."

"Oh, you are impossible! You are the most difficult man I've ever met!"

"Worse—than your father?" She hesitated, and he continued. "That at least is something."

She stammered. "Stephen, I do like you—very much. If it hadn't been for you . . . if you hadn't come when you did . . . why I might . . . I might be dead. I owe you so much. I am glad you are my cousin. We must become like brother and sister."

"Now *you* are being impossible! How can you repay me for what I've done in the way I have in mind if we become like brother and sister?"

Then he threw back his head and laughed, and to her surprise, so did she.

For a time Katherine and Stephen rode in silence. The sky was gray, and everything—the water, the granite cliffs, even the vegetation of the moors—seemed gray too. They rode to the tip of a hillock where the wind was sweeping up from the sea. Clutching her cloaks about her, Katherine was glad Stephen had given her his. Beneath them they saw the cliffs that edged the narrow beaches, The Queen's Light, and something else—something that had not been there the night Katherine had run away. A ship had foundered and now lay breaking apart on the reef.

"Snared by The Jaws," her father would say. The reef beneath. The Queen's Light had long been called The Jaws because at low tide when the rocks could be seen, they resembled the open jaws of a beast smiling wickedly.

Stephen urged his horse into a gallop, and as he sped away, Katherine remembered that, the night of the storm, The Queen's Light had gone out. Her father was probably feeling very low as a result, for he deemed it his personal responsibility to keep the lamp burning, especially on stormy nights. This would also explain why he hadn't searched for his runaway daughter. He had been occupied with trying to save the ship's crew and cargo.

When Katherine reached the seaside cliffs, she saw that Stephen had dismounted and was now climbing down the rocks to better view the ship. The tide was out, and she could see the rocks that held the vessel gleaming with spray. She remembered that night: the roaring wind, the rain, the cold. She thought of the unfortunate people who had sailed that ship, and she shuddered. After what seemed a long time Stephen returned, the expression on his dark face somber. She thought, This is the first time I've seen him truly serious.

"This must have happened the night I found you."

"And it explains why the Bodrugans did not return to their cottage and why my father did not have time to search for me."

"This was done deliberately."

"What? How can you say such a thing?"

"The Queen's Light was put out!"

"It was an accident," she said.

"A highly profitable one!"

"Are you saying that my father—"

"No, but someone—"

"You are being ridiculous!"

"Am I? You Cornish have profited for centuries off the wrecks your dangerous coastline causes. Perhaps there are some among you who do not think they happen often enough."

His accusations enraged her. Were they always to quarrel?

"I am Cornish! And I resent what you're saying! My father was a seaman—"

"So that's what you call him, and you called Robert Morley a pirate!"

"My father was a seaman, and he tries to prevent wrecks!"

Stephen leaped into his saddle and guided his horse beside hers. When she dug her heels into Gilly's flanks, he seized her horse by the reins. "Not so fast! It's not my habit to apologize, but I was unfair. Certainly this isn't your fault or your father's. It's just that I've been at sea in storms, and a sight like that"— he looked past her to the ship—"is not one of my favorites."

He frowned, and she saw that he was genuinely troubled.

"It's all right," she said. He turned his head and stared deeply into her eyes. She had the uncanny feeling he could read her mind and her heart. Then he smiled again, as if the very sight of her delighted him, as if he was happy just to have her with him. The wind ruffled his blue-black hair, and his teeth flashed white against his skin. He was chuckling, and she thought, He must be thinking up some new comment with which to torment me. Somehow she didn't mind, for when he looked at her like that, she felt wildly joyous.

There was something special about this man. He had the ability to evoke powerful feelings in her. She would either grow to love him or to hate him, but she could never be long indifferent to him. She thought, I must be very careful. He has been at Court and knows how to charm the most elegant of women. I am like a simple country maid—easy prey for someone like him. She remembered again the ring he carried with him to aid him in his seductions. I must be on my guard—always!

With their horses' hooves clattering on cobblestone, Katherine and Stephen rode into the courtyard of the castle. Two grooms dashed up to help them dismount. When one of the boys recognized Katherine, his mouth fell open like a door with a faulty hinge. "Why, it be her that be missing these two days past." He leered at Stephen, who was swinging himself to the ground.

Stephen towered over the two boys, and one look from him was enough to silence them. He helped Katherine dismount.

"You have a beautiful home," Stephen said casually, as if it were nothing out of the ordinary that she had disappeared for two days and was now returning with him. "I can see your father is a man of his age! He likes to display his wealth, and he has excellent taste."

Her father! Just the thought of him, and her temple pounded. Why must she always be so terrified of him?

She scarcely heard Stephen say, "I can see that Castle Cranston is not a proper castle at all but a modern structure built like so many of our grandest homes, in the shape of the letter *E*, to honor our Queen."

She heard herself murmur, "Father had it built before he married Mother."

"And after his, shall we say, successful career at sea."

He was trying to annoy her with his implication that her father had been a pirate, and for once she was thankful for the distraction. It kept her from thinking of how her father would punish her for running away.

Katherine led Stephen into the hall that was bustling with life. At first the two of them went unnoticed, for Sir Cranston was standing on the dais. His voice was booming. From time to time the men who stood listening beneath him would raise their mugs and cheer when they concurred with some statement he made. "Aye, my lord, aye!" Stephen's eyes drifted appreciatively over the hall as he noted the excessive ornamentation, the carved woodwork, the chandeliers, the vast expanse of oriel windows, the magnificent fireplaces, and the tapestries hanging on the walls. Truly this was a household of vast wealth.

There was a lull in Sir Cranston's speech. Katherine paled as her father paused in mid-sentence when his eyes fell on her. "Daughter?" he was looking behind her to Stephen. To her surprise, his face lighted into a smile, and he rushed from the dais to join them.

Julia, Clara, and Richard were racing ahead of him.

Julia was the first to reach them. She threw her arms around Katherine. "Darling, we've been worried—" Julia, Clara, and Richard surrounded Katherine, but Sir Cranston talked to Stephen as if he'd known him always.

Katherine thought, It's good to be home with my family even if Father does kill me.

Julia and Richard, Katherine's first cousins on her mother's side, had been adopted many years ago by Sir Cranston when their parents had been lost at sea. They were like brother and sister to her, as was Clara. Clara was no true relation, but the only survivor from a Spanish shipwreck some ten years before.

Richard smiled at Katherine in his kindly, big-brotherly way. She remembered suddenly that she was wearing his clothes, that she'd sneaked into his room and stolen them. Her cheeks flamed, but he said nothing to embarrass her. As she looked up at him—this cousin of hers who was ten years older, with his hair gleaming in the firelight like golden gorse and his skin tanned from working outdoors—she felt deeply grateful for his silence. He was so unlike Stephen, who would have tormented her unmercifully. Richard was almost a son to Sir Cranston, and Sir Cranston relied heavily upon him to help him manage his estate.

"Daughter!" Sir Cranston crushed her to him in a tight embrace. "I wouldn't have worried about you if I'd known you were in such good hands!" He eyed Stephen with approval, and Katherine felt stunned by his reaction. She'd thought he would be furious, but here he was welcoming her.

"I found her on the moors," Stephen said. "She'd become ill suddenly . . ."

Sir Cranston looked at the two of them, a curious, speculative gleam lighting his eyes, but Katherine, relieved that he was not angry, failed to notice it. Looking at her father, she was surprised at her feelings for him. When she'd run away, she'd thought she hated him. He had said she had to marry the man he chose. But now, seeing him again, she felt a strange joy in his presence, a fierce pride that such a man was her father. He stood before her smiling, genuinely glad to see her. He was not the same man who had screamed at her, who could casually destroy her happiness by forcing her to marry a man just because he was rich. He loved her, else why was he looking at her like that? He was tall, willful, arrogant, ready to bully all who opposed him, even her. He was an older version of the man Stephen would become. She thought him handsome for his years. His hair and beard that had once been black were now winged with silver; his dark eyes sparkled with affection. Surely this was not the same man who had said he would beat her senseless if she refused to marry Robert Morley.

She forgot their quarrel; she forgot Robert Morley. "Father," she said. "It's good to be back." Impulsively, she reached up and her lips brushed the coarse hairs of his beard.

He hugged her to him, and the breath went out of her. "And it's good to have you back! But we're being rude, girl! We must honor this kinsman of ours, Stephen San Nicholas, who has brought you back to me safe and sound! Watty! Jesse! Go down to the cellar and bring some sack! Fetch Mary and Sally! We will drink a round of toasts." He shouted so all could hear. "Everyone, this is Stephen San Nicholas, my kinsman from Devon! We must drink to his health!"

"Aye, my lord!" Cups were raised.

Sir Cranston slipped one of his massive arms about Stephen's shoulders. "It's good you found Katherine. For two days I've thought of nothing but this bloody wreck! The Queen's Light went out. Damnably odd. Everyone aboard was lost. Wreckers had already boarded her and stolen her cargo before I learned of it and mustered my men! And this isn't the first time this has happened of late. It seems almost as if—"

"We saw the ship," Stephen said.

Katherine marveled at the instant rapport between Stephen and her father. Her father was certainly behaving very strangely. He did not question her as to where she had spent the past two nights, or in whose company. Then Sally Bodrugan, very beautiful with her dancing black eyes and raven hair tied back with yellow ribbons, handed her a cup filled with wine, and she drank it. Sally placed a similar cup in Stephen's hand, and Stephen stared down at the pretty girl. Katherine saw his eyes linger on Sally's swaying hips as she moved away from him.

Soon they were surrounded by well-wishers, all happy for an excuse to forget the gloomy talk of wreckers and to taste that great gift to the English from the Spanish—sack. Cups filled with sugar, spices, and wine were rapidly emptied and refilled. Malmsey was served as well as metheglin, and other kinds of wines—gillyflower, elderberry, and blackberry.

Katherine noted that Jesse Bodrugan drank her ale as usual. One of Sir Cranston's arms now rested on Jesse's waist and he hugged her to him and kissed her on the lips. Wine made him grow amorous. Jesse laughed and pushed him away. Katherine eyed the pair with a twinge of resentment. She had heard—a most reliable source where gossip was concerned—from her maid that Sir Cranston had made his housekeeper, Jesse, his mistress and the mother of two of his illegitimate children even before he had married Katherine's mother. She could remember her maid's words, "There do be them that say, my Lady Kate, that Sally and Otto Bodrugan be your half sister and half brother, even though they be born before your mother come, and on the wrong side of the blanket." And indeed Sir Cranston did favor Otto and Sally as though they were special to him. They were black-eyed and black-haired, just as he had been in his youth. Still, he had never claimed them as his own.

Slackening his grip around Jesse's waist, Sir Cranston turned his attention once more to Stephen. "Let us retire to the winter parlor so that we can talk in private."

Little Watty, Sir Cranston's valet, led the way. A fire leapt in the grate, and above it, on the wall, hung a framed portrait of a much younger Sir Cranston. The artist had paid more attention to his costume than his features. In the picture Sir Cranston wore a padded jerkin of satin and red velvet glittering with jewels. Its puffed sleeves increased the expanse of his massive shoulders. Katherine had never liked the picture, for the eyes were watchful and seemed to follow one no matter where one stood in the room. On an easel in the corner of the room stood an unfinished portrait of Katherine. The artist had been forced to abandon his project because Katherine would never sit still for it.

"Jesse, you must bring us some of that capon and pie. They must be starved!" Sir Cranston said. "Katherine has grown as thin as a twig! And you know I've no taste for skinny women." He chuckled as the buxom housekeeper disappeared through the doorway.

Stephen and Sir Cranston began to talk, mostly of the sea, with Richard occasionally joining in. Again Katherine marveled at how quickly the two men had grown to like one another. Sir Cranston talked of his adventures at sea, and, to Katherine's surprise, Stephen had as many of his own to recount. He told them with a guarded reticence as if he carefully chose what he revealed about himself. She realized suddenly how little she knew of Stephen's background. She had spent two days and two nights with him, and he knew everything about her. Yet she knew very little about him. Strange that she'd never known she had such a cousin from Devon until her father had told her of him a fortnight ago. She determined to learn everything she could about this new cousin of hers.

Women certainly found him charming. Already Julia and Clara glowed every time he looked at them. All too often Sally appeared at his side, offering him a cake or sausage, refilling his goblet. It was obvious he found women as charming as they found him. When one of the girls spoke, he would lean forward and listen eagerly. He would smile and make some flattering remark, and they would blush. Katherine realized with a start that he was being much nicer to them than he had been to her. He spared them his barbed remarks. Occasionally, he looked at her, and there seemed to be a suppressed eagerness in his eyes. When he looked at her in that way, her pulse quickened, and she would turn away. No one had ever affected her as he did. She must be careful to keep her feelings hidden, for he would surely use them against her.

Talk turned to the sumptuous accommodations Sir Cranston had had prepared for Stephen. Katherine was surprised when she heard Stephen say, "My lord, you are most generous, too generous. I would prefer something simpler." His gaze drifted to Katherine. "On my way I developed a particular liking for a certain cottage, a fairly large one. Near The Queen's Light. It would be perfect for me."

"That be our cottage," Sally Bodrugan was saying, her eyes lighting with enthusiasm at the thought of the handsome stranger staying in one of their spare rooms. "We do have two sleeping rooms and a room in the loft. There be plenty of room with Otto gone so often and us at the castle."

Again Stephen looked at Katherine and smiled his too-knowing smile. She knew she was flushing.

"Then it is settled," Sir Cranston said. "You are our guest, and you can stay wherever you wish!"

"Thank you, my lord."

"Uncle," Julia timidly interrupted. "Uncle, today while you were busy with the wreck, Blake Finnley sent one of his servants over to tell us that he would be coming over tomorrow." Julia's cheeks brightened with color as Sir Cranston shifted his attention to her.

"Aye, is he now, I wonder—" Sir Cranston stroked his beard and looked at his niece intently. Her flush deepened.

Blake was coming tomorrow! Ordinarily such news would have thrilled Katherine, but today it didn't. She was suddenly aware that her father was looking at her, and so was Stephen. She rose and crossed the room to where the windows looked out upon the ornamental yews and flowering beds of the garden.

Stephen was quickly beside her. He bent his black head to hers and said in a low voice, "Your lover has an uncanny sense of timing. You are not home an hour and already we learn he is on his way."

Her temper flared. "He is not my lover!"

"Not yet. Not ever if I have anything to do about it!" He spoke harshly, and his eyes blazed with passion. "You'd better rest well tonight, madam. You look wan. His love may cool if he sees you looking thus."

Before she could reply, he'd crossed the room, and Sally Bodrugan was rushing to his side.

"I be happy to show you the way to our cottage," she said.

He lowered his dark head to her ear and whispered something that made her laugh merrily. Katherine looked away, for she could not bear the sight of them together.

Sir Cranston rose and joined his guest. "Stephen,

don't go just yet. We'll call Sally later to show you the way. Now I want to discuss something privately that is gravely important."

Katherine watched unhappily as the great doors closed behind them. How short-lived had been the joy of her homecoming. At least her father had not mentioned Robert Morley. That gave her time.

Blake was coming tomorrow, but she hardly cared. She looked out onto the garden, but she couldn't focus. All she could think of was Stephen and how his eyes had blazed with hatred. He took great pains to charm everyone but her. Why did he dislike her so? He had said she looked wan. Suddenly she had an overwhelming desire to run to her glass and see if her illness had made her ugly.

Oh, she must stop thinking of him and his insults. She must concentrate on Blake and how she would persuade him to help her escape from this marriage to Robert Morley. It had seemed so easy when she set out to run to him the other night. She had been so sure of her love for him and of his for her. But now it occurred to her that he had never once in all the months she had loved him even hinted at marriage.

Uneasily she remembered how her romance with Blake had begun. It had been she who had sought him out at first. After Christmas Blake had started calling on Sir Cranston at regular intervals to discuss business. Since the winter days were short, with little to interest her, she had grown bored. She had cornered Blake one crisp, cold afternoon and suggested she ride with him across the moors toward his estate. He hadn't wanted her to. In fact he had begged her not to, but she had insisted. After their first ride together, she'd made it her custom to wait for him and accompany him.

Slowly Blake had become as eager for her company as she had for his. At least, she had thought so. But, always, he'd been careful to hide his feelings for her from everyone else . . . especially her father. She must stop thinking about Blake's fear of her father. Blake loved her! And a man who loved a woman would let nothing stand in his way. She must stop doubting Blake and his love for her.

Stephen was right! She must rest so that she would look beautiful for Blake tomorrow. She would persuade him that he must elope with her, that he must save her from Robert Morley! She would show Stephen she didn't care at all what he thought! Or what he said! After all, she loved Blake! She did! But it was strange how often she thought of Stephen, and how easily he could upset her. Stranger still was the fact that she'd scarcely thought of Blake since she'd met Stephen. Still . . . tomorrow when she eloped with Blake she would show them all!

Chapter 4

Katherine's hair sparked as she ran her brush through it one last time. She smoothed her curls deftly into place and smiled at her reflection in the glass. She was too pale. Wan, Stephen had said. She rubbed her cheeks until they were rosy with color, and bit her lips. She lifted her green velvet cap, studded lavishly with pearls and emeralds, from the carved rosewood table and placed it on her head. The cap exactly matched her velvet gown. With its puffed, slashed sleeves and starched ruff the gown was much too formal for ordinary country wear, but today she wanted to look especially beautiful. She knew it flattered her, making her waist look tiny, and, because it was low-cut, revealed much of her ample bosom. Once more she smiled, dimpling. Then she tore her eyes from the dazzling reflection. Oh, she must hurry! Blake was already in the garden waiting for her! Mary had just brought his message.

She raced from her room, down the stairs, and out onto the terrace. There, directly in her path, stood Stephen. In one hand he carried a pair of leather gloves as if he were on his way to the gamekeeper's to fly a hawk. He had never looked more handsome.

His black hair was tossled, his eyes sparkling with mischief. He wore a beautifully embroidered light blue cambric shirt open at the throat, and close-fitting leather breeches. He had such a magnificent physique, such a narrow waist for one so tall and muscular. At the sight of her he smiled, and suddenly she felt very happy. His eyes drifted slowly from her face to her bosom to her waist, and his smile widened. Coloring, she wondered if he was looking at her that way to annoy her. She remembered his harsh words from the evening before, and her joy faded.

"It never ceases to amaze me what whalebone and leather can do for a woman's figure," he said, staring pointedly at her heaving bosom.

She was infuriated that he sought deliberately to embarrass her by referring to her undergarments—her leather corset and her whalebone farthingale.

"Why do you enjoy insulting me so much?" she cried.

"I thought I was complimenting you. This is, after all, the first time I've seen you dressed like a woman. You are absolutely bewitching. And I must ask, am I the reason you've taken such pains with your appearance?"

"No, you're not!" She was about to blurt out that Blake was waiting for her, but before she could, his face darkened and he said softly, "How could I have forgotten. But the sight of you so beautiful is enough to make the most intelligent of men become senseless. Blake is the one you're set on impressing. I saw him just now in the garden. I can't, for the life of me, figure out what you see in him. He's but a poor farm boy, afraid of his own shadow. Now don't puff up like an adder about to strike. It ruins your beauty. Don't stamp either! That's childish!"

"Oh! Oh! I don't know why I'm standing here taking this from you!"

"You'd rather chase after that stupid farm boy of yours!"

"He is not stupid!"

"He is stupid, and he isn't worthy of a girl like you!"

"At least he isn't vile-mannered, insulting, and—"

"Enough! I get the picture. It seems I am not the only one who can be insulting."

He moved toward her and she tried to dodge, but he was too swift. He seized her by the wrist and pulled her to him. "I'm going to let you go to him now—your farm boy with pretty manners—and learn once and for all that I am right about him. You are too beautiful, Katherine, to have to chase after a man who doesn't want you. I do want you."

"Only for some coarse interlude in your bed!"

"Is that what you think—that love with me would be coarse?" He released her, his eyes fierce. "Go to him, then, and discover for yourself how little he loves you!"

She ran past him toward her father's enclosed garden where Blake waited for her, pausing along the way to catch her breath and recover from her encounter with Stephen. Hurt and baffled, she wondered why he upset her so. A breeze blew her curls into her eyes, and when she raised her hand to brush them away, her fingers were damp. She was crying. For a long time she stood there trying to compose herself. She must forget Stephen! She must concentrate on how terrible marriage to Robert Morley would be and how she could charm Blake into rescuing her from that fate. But somehow Robert Morley and Blake no longer seemed important. She could think of nothing except Stephen.

"Katherine . . ."

Blake was running toward her. He took her hand in his and led her to a narrow bench in the most beautiful niche of the garden. They sat down amid brilliant hanging fuchsia and laburnum. Beneath them the sea sparkled. Katherine moved closer to Blake.

"Do not sit so close to me, Katherine," Blake said nervously, as he inched away from her. "Someone will see us from the castle."

As he moved away Katherine grew angry at his failure to act the part of an ardent lover. "It is only that he is so afraid of Father," she reassured herself.

Katherine glanced upward and scanned the large oriel windows that seemed like great eyes etched in the granite walls. "And let them look!" she said defiantly. "What do I care?" She saw Blake's eyes widen with alarm, and remembered suddenly that Blake liked gentleness, not boldness, in women. She paused, tilting her hazel eyes downward as if she were overcome with modesty. She continued more softly, "I remember a time when you did not care what Father or anyone thought."

His hand sought hers, which lay hidden in the emerald folds of her gown. "And I would not care now if your father had not specifically forbidden me to see you."

48

"My father! My father always ruins everything!" Looking at Blake, she had the strange sensation she was seeing him for the first time. His chocolate-brown eyes had grown larger with anxiety. He was perspiring heavily, and his chestnut curls lay in damp ringlets against his forehead. The thought occurred to her that Stephen would never be terrified of her father. Suddenly annoyed with Blake, she struggled to free her hand, but he held it tightly. From time to time he looked up at the castle walls, as if searching for some movement at a window. He looked absolutely terrified! Why, he wasn't manly! He was hardly more than a boy and certainly no match for Father. Instead of making her sympathetic to Blake, Katherine's observations only increased her annoyance with him.

Her eyes flashed like golden lights in a flame, and Blake held her hand all the more tightly, misinterpreting her emotion for passionate love instead of anger at his cowardice. Forgetting her father's threat for a minute, he smiled down at her with an utterly captivated look. As always when he looked at her that way, Katherine's heart melted, and she returned his smile.

Blake obviously thought her beautiful, and she remembered with pleasure how pretty she'd looked in her glass. She smiled up at him, and Blake continued to gaze at her like a spellbound puppy. She parted her full lips, inviting him to kiss her. After he kissed her, she would declare her love, reveal that her father was forcing her to marry Robert Morley, and demand that he save her from that fate.

Blake leaned forward, but he did not kiss her. Casting one last tortured look upon her lips, he abruptly rose as if to tear himself away.

"I must be going," he said. "My business with Sir Cranston is finished and if he finds me here with you after warning me only this morning—I don't know what he'll do."

Nothing seemed to work according to her plan. Katherine struggled not to betray the intensity of her frustration.

"Won't you at least kiss me? Just once?"

He pulled her fingers to his lips and kissed them gently.

"Not a kiss like that!" she cried indignantly. "Come with me. I know a private place where no one can spy on us."

She darted ahead of him and, peeping from behind an ornamental shrub, smiled her most coquettish smile.

"No one can see us here!" she cried breathlessly, taking his hands in hers. "We're too near the castle walls." She giggled. Blake's eyes drifted to the exact spot where her breasts swelled above the jewel-green cloth, and Katherine flushed. But he did not shower her with urgent kisses, as Katherine expected. Rather, he folded her gently into his arms, buried his head in her hair, and held her tightly for a long while.

"Katherine, there is something I must tell you. Something your father . . ."

Infuriated once more that Blake was not acting as she wanted him to, Katherine shrugged off his embrace. Before she could speak, Blake's velvet-brown eyes looked past her and widened with alarm. He spoke rapidly in hushed tones.

"There's your father with Julia and Clara. They're coming this way. Quick! Get down! We must not let them see us!"

"Father must know we're here," Katherine answered shortly. "Why else would he have come? He must have seen us from his closet window. Come, follow me. I know how best to handle him."

Katherine's pulse pounded like a mad drumbeat in her temple. She was angry with Blake for being so uncooperative and cowardly. Now her chance to persuade him to help her was lost. And all because of her father. She was suddenly furious with her father for always ruining her plans. With trembling fingers she smoothed back her hair and straightened the rumpled folds of her green velvet overskirt. Hurrying into the center of the garden with a scarlet Blake cowering at her heels, she hoped she didn't look as guilty or fearful as she felt. Father despised cowardice.

"Ah, dear Katherine," Sir Cranston's voice boomed. "I thought we might find you here. Enjoying yourselves, I see."

Sir Cranston's black eyes took in every detail of the guilty pair's appearance—the disarray of Blake's apparel, his shamefully red complexion. Nor did he fail to note the flame of anger in Katherine's cheeks. He smiled down at his daughter, but she did not think it a kind smile. She knew he had come into the garden deliberately to catch her with Blake.

"I'm on my way to the gamekeeper's to see if

Stephen and Richard are making any progress with that new hawk," Sir Cranston said. "But before I go I'll have a final word with Blake about that little matter we were just discussing."

Blake winced uncomfortably at Sir Cranston's words, remembering too well the little matter they had just discussed.

"But come, boy! Let's leave the girls to enjoy the garden and idle chatter." To Katherine he added: "And, Daughter, I want to see you and your cousin Julia in my closet within the hour. Don't keep me waiting!"

Katherine and her two friends seated themselves upon the same narrow bench she had recently shared with Blake and spread their billowing skirts before them.

Katherine was too disturbed to enjoy the beauty of the blossoming garden. Nor did she listen as Julia and Clara discussed the upcoming May Day festivities and gaily speculated on who would be selected May Queen. Normally such conversation would have interested her, but today she stared blankly ahead in stony silence.

Something was wrong. Stephen had said she would discover how little Blake loved her, and Blake had been different today. He had been on the verge of telling her something important when her father had come into the garden. And her father—he too had acted strangely, as if he knew something that she did not.

The sun shone brilliantly, warming the land and turning the sea into a shimmering body of azure jewels, while the cool sea breeze made the girls' hair dance gently at the napes of their necks. But Katherine was oblivious to it all as she sat lost in thought.

"Katherine, dear, you are not listening," Julia said tremulously. "But then why should you be interested in what we're saying—we've been over the same ground so many times."

"It is the curse of living in the country," Clara said. Her fingers reached above her forehead to pat into place the raven coils piled high on top of her head in an elaborate coiffure. "Nothing eventful ever happens, so we must bore ourselves silly talking about the same thing over and over again. It's no wonder Katherine is so distant. We've said nothing today we haven't said every day for the past month."

"And as usual, we have decided that you, dearest cousin, shall be named May Queen," Julia said fondly.

Katherine managed a smile. Normally this statement would have delighted her, for she had been hoping against hope that this year she would be chosen May Queen. Of late she had relished a certain vision of herself enthroned on the village square as her Royal Grace, the May Queen, costumed in a gown of white satin overlaid with gold netting. In her vision she saw the crowd part, and Blake walk toward her to place a garland of golden laburnum in her hair. She smiled at him and then stepped down from her throne and took his hands in hers. He would kneel to pay homage to her and then she and Blake would dance and dance beneath the Maypole, and everyone—even her father—would see how much they loved one another. But today, Katherine was not in the mood to dream this favorite dream.

"Well, if they don't choose me this year, I'll be too old next year," she said.

Clara laughed. "Nonsense! What's more likely is that you'll be married to that Robert Morley long ere we see another May Day!"

The mention of marriage immediately produced a profound change in the countenances of both Julia and Katherine. Julia smiled—a strangely radiant smile —while Katherine's expression darkened.

Yes, Katherine thought. Father has every intention of marrying me off to that monster, and soon. It wasn't fair! Oh, why did the old have such power over the lives of the young?

If only she could persuade Blake to propose marriage, to elope. But today when she had had the perfect opportunity, she had failed to accomplish this. When would she get to see Blake alone again? How could she make him forget his fear of her father? She would have to be clever and plan carefully.

"Katherine, dear," Julia's trembling voice interrupted Katherine's thoughts. "I don't know how to tell you this . . ."

Annoyed at this interruption, Katherine turned to her cousin. Julia's violet eyes, too large and timid, were imploring.

"Well, what is it, Julia?"

"Clara did just mention marriage, and you know Blake Finnley has been a frequent visitor at Cranston Castle this winter."

A nerve spasmed in Katherine's neck. It seemed suddenly that Julia could read her mind. "Really, Julia, I hardly think my father would consider Blake as a husband for me. You know he has said I must marry Robert Morley," she replied as coolly as she could.

Julia was only slightly relieved with this answer. "I'm glad to hear that because, well, I love Blake." She hesitated. "And he loves me," she rushed on. "He has asked me to marry him this very week. And you must, on no account, tell Blake I've confided this to you. He has asked me several times to keep our love a secret from you. You see, he is afraid that you might tell your father. He's afraid to ask your father for my hand. We've been seeing each other all winter. Oh, I've grown to love him so! I thought . . ." She hesitated once more, looking uncertainly into Katherine's now clouded eyes. "Well, I thought you might help me to talk to your father. You've a way with him others haven't. Oh, Katherine, I love Blake with all my heart! I'll just die if Sir Cranston forbids this marriage!" Julia sat back, relaxing from the ordeal of her long speech.

Clara pressed Julia's hand warmly and said, "Julia, dear, I am so happy to hear this news. I wish you every happiness."

Julia was radiant. In her exuberance at having finally unburdened her heart's contents to her dear cousin and friend she failed to notice the effect of her words upon Katherine.

Katherine was chewing on lips that had turned a deadly bluish white. She hid her trembling hands beneath the heavy folds of her gown. Her pulse seemed to rush, stop, and then rush once more.

If Blake had come into the garden that instant, Katherine would have gladly murdered him on the spot. He had toyed with her affections, made a fool of her. Her emotions were in violent turmoil. Angry and hurt, she remembered Blake's pretty lies—how they had taken late afternoon rides upon the moors, how he had gently kissed her. She remembered Stephen's warning and became more infuriated because he had been right.

Stephen was probably already laughing at her. Did anyone besides him know of her love for Blake—someone who could have seen them on the moors? Were they whispering to each other that Blake had made love to the fast one while he talked marriage to the proper one? She writhed at the thought. What a fool she had been. She wondered if he had dared to tell Julia of his dalliance, but as she gazed into her cousin's shining eyes, she knew the answer.

Julia must never know. Although Katherine yearned to confront Blake and shout out her rage at him, she could not sacrifice the last vestige of dignity that was still hers. Pride overruled her rage and hurt, and she knew she had to pretend she was happy at Julia's news.

"When we see your father this afternoon, do you think you could mention to him that Blake wants to marry me?" Julia asked. "It would be so much easier if you were there with me. I could speak to him myself . . ." Julia looked appealingly into Katherine's eyes.

How could she help Julia wed the man . . . Katherine replied shortly, "Oh, of course, Julia! Of course!"

Katherine rose abruptly and strode to her father's enclosed garden with its pond and marble statuary that had been modeled after the garden of Hampton Court. The flower beds at her feet were bordered with rosemary, lavender, and marjoram. A fountain played at the center. How like her father to impose order here in this setting of wild beauty. He always imposed his will and that was why her heart was breaking today, that was why Blake had proposed to Julia and not to her. Blake was afraid of opposing her father's will. Katherine thought of Blake's arms around her. And Stephen laughing. She cried out and quickly clamped her fingers tightly over her lips. Her eyes blurred, and she ran to the furthest edge of the well-ordered garden. Gazing beyond the garden, she found solace in the grim wildness of the moor, which sloped down to the treacherous marshes on one side and the rugged cliffs above the sea on the other.

"Katherine, dear, where are you? Oh there you are." Her golden hair coming loose from its net, and her voluminous skirts swirling about her frail, almost childlike body, Julia hurried toward her. "Darling, I haven't said anything wrong, have I? I've upset you. Why, you've been crying." Julia's hand touched Katherine's cheek lovingly and brushed back a strand of copper hair, Katherine pulled away. "There, there, forget I ever said anything," she soothed. "You don't have to talk to your father. I'm grown. I can manage myself."

"I don't mind at all, Julia. It's just that I've got an awful headache. Sitting in the sun does that to me sometimes. And when I think of you marrying, and leaving me—even if you are so happy . . . And I think

57

of myself and Robert Morley and of my leaving you and Cornwall—it all upsets me." She dabbed at her eyes.

"Of course it does, darling." Julia's eyes grew moist. "I've been so selfish, thinking of my own happiness instead of realizing how all this is affecting you."

Katherine rubbed her temples as if they ached and was about to speak when footsteps crunched onto gravel, and Clara and Stephen approached, laughing together over something Stephen was saying.

"Ladies, I grew weary at the gamekeeper's, for hawks are not nearly so amusing as three beautiful women." Glancing at Katherine, he noticed her reddened eyes and tear-stained cheeks. To Katherine's surprise he became serious at once. "Do you mind," he said to Julia and Clara, "if I talk to my cousin alone? We will join you in the castle directly."

Katherine was sure he was anxious to gloat. When Stephen and she were alone, she said, "You must be very happy, very, very happy." She burst into tears.

"It does not necessarily follow that I am happy when you are unhappy," he said kindly. "Even when you're unhappy because of another man."

She blinked back her tears. He slipped an arm around her waist, and for some reason she did not pull away. "You will get over him more quickly than you think."

"But Father will make me marry Robert Morley!" She was sobbing once more.

"A fate worse than death, surely," he murmured.

"I don't want to marry a man I don't love."

"Arranged marriages are commonplace. I was once so married myself."

"You were?" she found to her surprise that she was no longer crying, for she was too interested in Stephen and what he was saying.

"Yes. Many years ago." He hesitated, and his eyes darkened with some unpleasant memory. "It was disastrous. I vowed I would never marry again."

"Then you understand what I am feeling now?"

"Yes, I do, and I won't let it happen. I will find a way to help you."

"But Father?"

"I said I will help you when the time comes. For now I have business that occupies me."

Katherine realized again how little she knew about Stephen. "What is the exact nature of this . . . this business that brings you to Cornwall?"

"Ah, curiosity, thy name is woman." He was grinning at her.

"You won't tell me?"

"No."

"Then you must be a pirate or something illegal!"

He threw back his head and laughed. "Do you call everyone a pirate?"

"You have been to sea."

"And so has your father." She flushed, and he continued. "I ran away to sea when I was quite young to escape a tragic past." His voice was no longer light, his gaiety had fled.

"How mysterious—this past of yours. But then everything about you is mysterious."

"I hardly think it is a question of being mysterious.

It is just that you Cornish are so snoopy, always prying into a fellow's business."

"Well, if you didn't have something to hide you'd—"

"So you are determined to believe I'm a pirate?" He laughed again, his good humor restored. "I'm afraid not—much too dangerous. I prefer a fresh suit of clothes, a beautiful woman, and a soft bed, which brings us back to you and me. Do you know how beautiful you are with your pale skin, your golden eyes, and your hair, bright with sunlight, blowing in the wind. Why not find consolation for your broken heart in my bed?"

"Stephen! Why do you always spoil everything? You were being so nice."

"And you like me when I'm nice?" He watched her with great interest, as if her answer was very important to him.

"A little," she said at last.

His eyes were on her lips. With catlike grace he bent down quickly and kissed her full on the mouth. For an instant she felt giddy and clung to him. He pulled himself away.

"I think," he said, "you like me much more than a little."

As always when she found herself in his company, she felt excited. He smiled at her and offered her his arm, which she accepted. She felt strangely light-hearted for one so recently jilted.

"Come," he said. "You don't want to keep your father waiting."

Chapter 5

Needle in hand, Clara, the only calm one of the three girls, sat near a window in Katherine's vast bedchamber where the light was best, slowly working at the loom. The canvas was set up on a huge frame, and she worked from a picture that Katherine's mother had sketched in her youth. The design depicted Elizabeth's coronation, an event Katherine's mother had personally witnessed. It would take years to complete the tapestry, and hundreds of skeins of silk had been stored away. Katherine found work at the loom tedious, and avoided it whenever possible.

Julia paced in front of the massive fireplace like a caged cat, while Katherine, chewing on a ragged fingernail and gazing with unseeing eyes out the window, stood behind Clara. The weather had worsened suddenly. Dark clouds that had lurked on the horizon all day now blotted out the sun. The jewellike sea had become a frothy gray turbulence. Katherine's own heart seemed as turbulent as that sea. Not so long ago she had been sure of Blake and his love for her. Then Stephen had come into her life, and Blake had jilted her. She should feel brokenhearted, devastated, but strangely enough, she did not. As if she were a new person, she no longer knew herself and could not count on how she would react to anything. She was deeply angry at Blake, but if she loved him, she should feel more than anger, and she did not.

Her reaction to Stephen was even more difficult to comprehend. When she was with him she felt strangely stimulated. She even enjoyed their quarrels. Still, Stephen was virtually a stranger, and he would walk out of her life as abruptly as he had entered it. She would be foolish to attach any importance to her feelings for him. But how could she think of Stephen when, in minutes, she would have to face her father.

Doubtless her father would bring up his plans for her marriage. She should be gathering her wits to think of a way to change his mind. Marry Robert Morley, a murderer! How could her father plan such a horror? She flinched suddenly as she bit through her nail and pierced the soft flesh of her finger.

Julia shivered violently and moved closer to the fire. The sun had scarcely been gone half an hour and already the room was damp and chilly. Julia shuddered once more, and plucked nervously at the lace fringes on her handkerchief.

"Julia!" Katherine said sharply, as she crossed the bedroom to her cousin, who was wringing her hands in anxiety. "What have you done to your poor handkerchief? Let me look at it. Why, you've practically torn it to shreds." All the delicate lace which had been so carefully crocheted by Julia's long-dead mother was in ribbons.

Julia glanced at the handkerchief and became instantly remorseful. "Oh, how could I do such a thing?

It's just that I'm so nervous I don't know what I'm doing!"

"Terrified is a better word," Katherine retorted, offering no sympathy. "Why on earth should you fear my father? Didn't he take you and Richard in, feed, clothe, raise, and educate you? Surely that isn't such a terrible thing to do?"

"No, no. I never meant to sound ungrateful. He's been wonderful. It's just that . . ." Julia stopped, groping unsuccessfully for the right word.

"Well, calm down! You know Father despises cowardice. You're certainly not going to make a good impression on him if you go in trembling like a leaf."

Katherine hated to admit—even to herself—her intense dread of her father. Her fears made her unusually cross with Julia.

But Julia was somewhat comforted by her cousin's show of courage. "Oh, Katherine, if only I were as brave as you!" Her eyes shone in admiration. "Blake has told me so many times how much he admires your boldness."

Katherine flushed and said irritably, "Let's go. Father will be in his study now."

Sir Cranston was not yet in his closet, but neither girl felt relieved that they could for a short while longer postpone the dreaded interview.

Poor Julia was terror-stricken. In spite of the circumstances, Katherine felt genuinely sympathetic toward her cousin.

It was obvious that Julia was madly in love with Blake and that Sir Cranston's decision about her marriage—a decision he would make hastily and seemingly with little thought—would either make her the happiest or saddest woman on earth.

As she waited for her father's arrival, Katherine's own tension mounted. Gazing about the room, his room, she almost felt his presence. She had always hated this room because she associated it with him and with all the times during her childhood he had summoned her here to discipline her. Although no longer a child, she was still here, waiting for his command.

Truly it was a beautiful room! Her father appreciated beauty, his tastes running to the lavish, the ostentatious. Enormous oriel windows looking out onto the sea spanned the width of the room. Two walls were paneled with oak and lined with shelves containing Sir Cranston's precious books. At the furthest end of the library stood the elegant fireplace, its overmantel of delicately carved marble towering twenty feet above the two logs that crackled merrily in the fireplace beneath.

His room like all of his possessions was immaculately kept. Katherine attributed her father's orderliness to his determination to control.

I'm no more to him than that inkstand, she thought, something that he intends to make use of, as if I have no feelings, no desires of my own.

Her gaze drifted to the sea. Rising out of the mists and crowning a spit of cliff, stood the tower that housed The Queen's Light.

Sir Cranston's tiny valet, Watty Godolghan, entered the room noiselessly. He smiled at the two girls and then quietly went about his duties, changing a candle here, flicking a speck of dust there, all with a reverence that was oddly touching. Katherine was reminded that her father was capable of inspiring intense devotion in his servants.

Yet Watty was not just another of her father's servants. He was different, special in a terrible sort of way. Watty was *his* servant, just as this room was *his* room. Rumor had it that Watty was a carnival murderer her father had saved from the gallows. Watty *owed* his master more than the other servants owed him. Watching Watty, Katherine knew that he belonged to her father as much as any human being could ever belong to another. Sir Cranston had only to command and Watty would obey. Even though Katherine herself did not fear Watty—he had been like a gentle nursemaid to her after her mother had died—she knew that the other servants feared and avoided him.

Sir Cranston insisted that Watty accompany him on any mission of danger because Watty was fiercely heroic. "Watty, he be afraid of nothing—be it living or dead," she had heard the servants say. And Watty had rescued Clara from The Jaws.

Katherine remembered that stormy night years ago when sea and granite had broken apart a vessel named *La Dama Misteriosa*. At first the villagers had thought she was but another ship who had sailed in Spain's Armada, but she had carried gold and silver and no cannon. The townspeople and Sir Cranston's servants had lined the shore like vultures, waiting for something of value to wash into the shallows. The night had been too savage even for them to risk venturing out to the distressed ship. But Watty had plunged into the waters and brought back a small passenger, a half-drowned child strapped to a piece of planking—Katherine's beloved Clara.

"Watty, do you think Father will be here soon?"

"Aye. He were with Master Richard at the gamekeeper's. That haggard Master Richard were so keen to fly did not return to the gauntlet proper-like. One talon missed the glove and tore a nasty gash in Master Richard's arm."

"Oh, no!" Julia gasped. "Sir Cranston tried to stop Richard from flying that hawk!"

"Master Richard, he do have a strong mind, if you don't mind me saying it. And it were that haggard or none, it were. But don't you be worried, Miss Julia, your brother claims it were no more than a cat's scratch. Jesse Bodrugan be with them now to bandage his cut and apply her special mixture of herbs. They will be here any minute."

"I'm relieved to hear it," Julia said.

"Anyhow, Sir Cranston and Master Richard be in a jolly mood, having quaffed enough ale during the bandaging to make ten men merry." Watty chuckled to himself.

Katherine hoped that this last statement meant her father wouldn't be as impossible as he usually was.

Laughter was Sir Cranston's herald. Richard and he entered the study, still smiling over their latest piece of wit. Katherine thought her father's sense of humor crude, and she hoped he would spare her his jokes.

Seeing Katherine and Julia, both men laughed, so delighted were they at the prospect of retelling their morning's misadventure to a receptive feminine audience. In spite of their apprehension about the coming interview with Sir Cranston, the girls listened attentively to the tale and struggled to suppress their smiles at the places where Sir Cranston embellished Watty's version.

"But we've wasted enough time discussing that poxy haggard," Sir Cranston said at last. "We'll leave that feathered devil to the gamekeeper for a week or so and he'll be fit enough, I'll warrant." He stroked his beard and smiled down at the girls. "And now let's get on with the reason I've sent for the two of you." Katherine's gaze locked with his. "It seems to me you're both of a marrying age . . ." Julia gasped and clutched her heart as if she suddenly felt faint, but Sir Cranston took no notice. He was still staring at his daughter. "I've had a most interesting interview with Blake." Katherine flushed hotly and looked away. Then she glared back at him defiantly, and he laughed aloud. He liked boldness, especially in his daughter.

"All winter," Sir Cranston continued, "Blake has been visiting me on business matters, but for some time I've suspected his visits to have a double meaning." Here, he paused to look at Julia, whose eyes were wide with fear. "Or perhaps a triple meaning." He eyed Katherine. "Ah, to say the latest, I've been more than a little curious to discover his intentions." His black eyes flashed with amusement.

Sir Cranston was the only one enjoying himself. Watty was furiously arranging the logs in the fireplace. Julia was wild-eyed with alarm, and Katherine, who was scarlet, stared fixedly at the toe of her green slipper. Poor Richard observed both girls sympathetically, for he knew from experience what it was to squirm uncomfortably at Sir Cranston's words.

After what seemed an interminable time Sir Cranston said, "Well, I won't prolong the suspense. This very afternoon Blake has asked for Julia's hand in marriage." A radiant Julia gasped at this unexpected news. "What say you to this match, Niece?"

"Oh, yes, yes, yes!"

"And Richard, will you have Blake as a husband for your little sister?"

"Yes, I think it an excellent match, especially as I see how happy Julia is."

"Then, it's settled, unless you, Daughter, can offer some objection." His voice was mocking.

"Certainly I have no objection," Katherine retorted hotly.

"Then it is settled. Blake will make a good husband, and I will provide a generous dowry. Julia, child, come here and let me congratulate you."

Julia was radiant with joy as she stepped forward, amazed that her heart's desire had been accomplished so easily and so swiftly. One never knew what Sir Cranston's reaction would be.

Her uncle embraced her and kissed her affectionately. All traces of mockery vanished from his voice as he said, "I'm very proud of you, and I verily hope this marriage makes you a happy woman. I shall talk to Blake as soon as possible. We shall announce the wedding at the May Day festivities. Watty, go down to the cellar and bring some sack. Fetch Jesse and Mary and Sally. We need to drink a round of toasts. It is not every day we have such news. And Richard, we are going to put this estate in top shape before the wedding, if it means working day and night to do it. I don't want to entertain the entire countryside with everything in a shambles. Jesse will supervise all the renovations within the house, but it will be up to you to oversee the external improvements."

Soon the study was filled with well-wishers, all happy for any excuse to celebrate. Katherine could not help noticing that neither Sally Bodrugan nor Stephen was present.

Sack was served along with elderberry wine. Goblets were rapidly emptied and refilled. Katherine's anger ebbed as she drained her second cup of elderberry wine.

Sir Cranston laughed aloud and said, "Today I am a happy man, almost as happy as I was the day I sailed home, having helped vanquish those bloody Spaniards and their Armada! The devils said they'd whip us in a day, and who went to the bottom of the sea? Ha! Ha!"

"We must set a date for this wedding," Jesse said.

"Patience, woman! All in good time!" Sir Cranston answered, feeling slightly put out that Jesse had interrupted his oft-told tale of how he and other English sailors like him had stood against Spain's Armada and saved England from the Spaniards and the terrors of the Inquisition. But suddenly he smiled as if it suited him well that she had interrupted him. He eyed Katherine slyly. I've more news yet," he continued. "I've decided that Julia will be our May Queen. It is only fitting that we honor our bride."

Richard swooped Julia into his arms and kissed

her. "Your uncle doubly honors you, Sister, with his approval of your marriage and now with this. Sir, you are too generous!"

"Nonsense!" Sir Cranston boomed. "It is only fitting to honor one who has always obeyed me." He stared pointedly at Katherine, who knew he was naming Julia queen because she, Katherine, had defied him when she had refused to marry Robert Morley.

The servants clamored to be near the radiant Julia. None of them noticed Katherine edge noiselessly toward the windows. The rain was pounding now, and the rising wind smudged heavy droplets against the panes of glass so that the sea beneath was a blur of gray. Soon it would be dark. She raised a hand to the glass and absently traced the pattern of an aimless rivulet that crisscrossed the windowpane.

"Things haven't been going very well for you lately, and I've missed your beautiful smile," Richard said gently. Katherine started, for she had thought herself alone at the window. He took her hand in his and pressed it. "I've news that will make you smile once more."

She should not have been surprised to find him there. All her life he had been like an older brother to her and she had often turned to him when hurt or confused.

"I don't believe I'll smile today." Still, she was mildly curious.

"You are to be Maid Marian in the May Day festival, and you will be the most beautiful Maid Marian we've ever had."

"Maid Marian! How can you expect that news to make me happy? I wanted to be the queen! But, no,

Julia is to have everything!" Katherine blurted out as a rush of resentment toward her father swept her.

Richard ignored her outburst and continued calmly, "Your father sought only to honor the bride."

"My father seems to think of pleasing everyone but me," Katherine said sulkily. "Of course I don't blame Julia for what has happened. Everything is Father's fault!"

"Why don't you look at the bright side? Before long you will realize that Blake could never be the right man for you. Besides, you're perfect for the part of Maid Marian. The May Queen sits on a throne all day, but you'll be in the procession and dance around the Maypole." He bent low and whispered in her ear, "No one dances as gracefully as you."

She knew Richard was deliberately trying to lift her spirits, but, in spite of a certain perverse desire to dwell on the recent injustices she had suffered, she responded to her cousin's flattery with a smile.

"You're just saying that because you're the kindest, most softhearted man I've ever known! You don't really think I dance more gracefully than the other girls!"

"Of course I do! No one will even look at the queen while you're dancing, for no one will be able to take his eyes off you."

Katherine's tremulous smile brightened as she envisioned herself swirling beneath the Maypole.

"You see, I have made you smile."

"Yes, I suppose you have." She squeezed his hand affectionately.

"I'm glad. But come, let's join the others." He

cupped her elbow with his hand and led her across the room.

The servants were talking about one of Otto Bodrugan's latest escapades, and his mysterious disappearance over a fortnight ago.

Sir Cranston laughed indulgently. "I was very like him when I was his age," he said.

Katherine was reminded anew that some people believed Sir Cranston was in truth Otto's father.

The servants embraced Julia one last time, and she, whom the wine had made sentimental, wept with joy.

Sir Cranston once more focused his attention on his daughter. His dark eyes gleamed faintly as he said, "Daughter, stay after the others have gone. I mean to have a word with you."

All too soon the servants returned to their chores, and Julia, an arm linked through Jesse's, the two of them discussing plans for the wedding, left also.

Watty said, "I be on my way to light The Queen's Light before it be night and the weather worse." He pulled the doors shut behind him, and Katherine was alone with her father.

Chapter 6

Lightning scribbled across the darkening sky, followed closely by a roar of thunder. Another burst of brilliance and sound, like a gigantic fireworks display, set the world ablaze again. Sir Cranston, his silvery brows furrowed into a single line above his eyes as he watched the storm with growing consternation, sighed heavily. He turned to face his daughter.

"I don't like it. Another storm so soon after the other." He crossed himself quickly and offered a silent prayer.

Katherine knew her father, like most seamen of his time, was very superstitious. Whenever anything worried him, he made the sign of the cross and prayed for luck. It was a habit that betrayed he had been born into the old religion and still followed it, even though he was a Protestant by law. The Queen, as leader of the Protestant faith, suspected non-Protestants of being potential enemies, making it dangerous to worship in the old faith.

But when had her father feared danger? Katherine knew that services were held behind closed doors in the chapel and that beneath the altar cloth there was a hidden door concealing images and utensils used in the celebration of mass.

"The weather does look ominous," she agreed, putting all thoughts of religion from her mind.

"The thunder sounds like all the cannon of a gunboat going off at once, but enough talk of the storm. Daughter, it will doubtless please you to know that, of late, you've often been in my thoughts." Katherine squirmed uneasily. "I'm proud of you, Katherine. You've grown very beautiful, and it seems a pity to waste such beauty."

"What is this leading up to, Father?"

"Jesse tells me you're an excellent housekeeper—when you set your mind to it. You'll make your husband a good wife. In short, Daughter, it's time we settled this matter about your marriage to Robert Morley."

"We, Father? Am I, after all, to have some choice in the matter?"

"Why, why yes. Of course you will, my dear. Your feelings will be considered." He seemed uneasy, as if he felt the conversation was beginning to take a wrong turn, as it often did when Katherine was involved.

"I don't wish to marry at all," she declared flatly.

"Such an idea is preposterous!"

"I don't think marriage would suit me."

"Ridiculous! What does a seventeen-year-old girl know of marriage? Of course you must marry. You were meant for marriage. No one in the county can take his eyes off you. Witness that young puppy Blake. Oh yes, I know all about Blake and so does everyone else. He's made a fool of you! But no matter . . .

it but proves my point. You're a lusty wench and overripe for marriage."

"So you're marrying Blake to Julia so I can't have him."

"Katherine, why must you be so childlike and blame everything on me? Blake wants to marry Julia, and she wants him. Let them alone. They're spineless weaklings—both of them. I don't mean anything unkind by that. They're gentle people. They're not for the likes of us. Why, if you were married to Blake, you'd be wretched in six months' time. Now don't cloud up on me, girl! I know what I'm talking about. You'd bully him, and then despise him all the more because you could. You need a man, not some puppy."

"I loved Blake!"

"Puppy love!"

"What do you know of love? You're old—"

"Old enough to have loved and to have seen loves such as yours and Blake's grow sour with time. One day you'll thank me for saving you from such a fate."

"Never!"

"You'll thank me for finding you a proper husband, a man who can handle you."

"Robert Morley?"

"Yes!" Sir Cranston said. "Robert Morley, scion of the most illustrious shipping family from Plymouth. What appreciation do I get for making such a brilliant match for you? Defiance!"

"They are pirates like you! I don't wonder you'd approve such a family when our Queen makes heroes of men like Francis Drake and you. A fine example she sets. She makes heroes of murderers!"

"Careful, girl. Do you grow weary of having a head on your shoulders? It's treason you speak."

"I don't care! Losing my head would be no worse than marrying Robert Morley. How can you want to marry me to him? He murdered his first wife when he tired of her exactly in the manner that Robert Dudley murdered Amy Robsart when he thought to wed the Queen. And you—you'd marry me to such a man?"

"Robert Morley never murdered anyone. I've been to Plymouth. I've met him, and because I have, I know he would never kill his own wife. Rumors like this are impossible to disprove."

"It would seem they are more than rumors. His own father banished him for ten years."

"Even fathers can make mistakes, as you yourself have told me often enough. I believe Robert was falsely accused, and at any rate, ten years estrangement from all he holds dear should more than atone for his crime, if crime it were!"

"I cannot agree. Nothing but his death could atone for taking a life."

"You are being ridiculous, Katherine! You know nothing of Robert Morley, nothing. And I do. I've met him, talked with him, grown to like him. Yes, he was banished. And what did he do? He made something of himself. He wrested a fortune from the sea like I did."

"He was a pirate!"

"A privateer! And all with the Queen's consent. They say he stands high in her favor and is often at Court while his fool of a father is out of favor. He is a man who makes his own destiny, a man I would be proud to have as my son-in-law. Nay, the man I *shall* have as my son-in-law. The two of you will breed well. Your children, *my* grandchildren, will be of sturdy stock."

"I find your farmer's talk of breeding coarse. The man's a murderer!"

"Know this, Daughter. Whatever he is, he'll be your husband."

"I will never marry him, Father. Never!"

It was good, after all, that Sir Cranston had drunk as much wine as he had. Had he not, his temper would have erupted into one of his rages which made him the man most feared throughout the countryside.

He managed calmly, "Katherine, I have never yet taken the strap to you, but, I swear, I will if you refuse to marry this man. I will lock you in your room so that you can't pull any more of your tricks, like running away. Did you really think you could run so far that I would not track you down? Ha! Ha! Had you run to the furthest tip of Scotland, I would have brought you back and married you to this man. Do you think I want to force you to marry against your will? Well, I don't. But remember: it is my right. I know what is best for you. You are mine to dispose of where I will. You will be the wife of Robert Morley, and I'll not discuss this with you any longer. Begone!"

For one long moment father and daughter glared coldly at one another. The air between them was brittle with hatred. Then it seemed to Katherine that something inside of her shattered like glass. She burst into uncontrollable tears. Sir Cranston turned his back to her and stared angrily into the lavender-orange swirl of fire in the grate.

The casement windows trembled as a spear of light like a giant's harpoon hurtled into the sea. Thunder rumbled continually where water met sky in a hazy line. As if she desired to be heard above the noise of the storm, Katherine sobbed more loudly. Her father shifted his weight restlessly from one leg to the other. When he could stand the sounds of her weeping no longer, he pivoted suddenly to face her. Through the blur of her tears, Katherine scanned his face for any trace of sympathy but found none. His black eyes were hard; his lips set in a thin, determined line. How well she knew that look. When he spoke, his voice vibrated with impatience.

"Daughter, I thought I told you to leave me."

Katherine did not reply. Instead she sobbed convulsively. A knock sounded faintly at the doors, but neither Sir Cranston nor Katherine heard it. The doors swung open and Stephen San Nicholas stepped swiftly into the room. He had been smiling when he opened the doors, but at the sight of Katherine's swollen face and Sir Cranston's scowling one, he became grave.

Had Katherine been in a better mood she would have laughed at the sight of him, for he had changed clothes since she'd seen him last. He was now dressed in the ridiculous attire of a Court dandy. In spite of herself, she stared unblinkingly at him. Her vision cleared and, for one moment, she forgot why she was crying. Her jawline slackened. Why, people would think him a fool. They would laugh at him if he made a practice of dressing that way.

Stephen wore a doublet of deep turquoise Genoa velvet frothed with gold lace and embroidery. The rich color seemed to deepen the blackness of his hair. He wore a pair of ribbed Venetian hose cut very full and ballooning at his hips before tapering to his knees, which gave him the shape of a melon. From his shoulders swung a short, perfumed Spanish cloak of the finest leather, trimmed to match his doublet with gold embroidery and lace. Beneath the cloak, the gems and pearls of his heavy necklace glimmered. But the most ridiculous part of his apparel was the giant starched ruff his chin rested upon. Twelve inches of cambric as gauzy as a spider's web stood out stiffly from his neck.

Yes, the rough men of Cornwall would laugh at him if he made it a habit to dress in such a manner. They would make crude jokes— "His head above his ruff be very like John the Baptist's upon the platter." But they would do well to laugh behind his back rather than to his face, because even when he dressed as a dandy, there was something almost threatening about him. He was so tall, so massive. His broad shoulders were thickly laced with muscle. His foppish frills and scents, in sharp contrast to his masculinity, only intensified one's awareness of it. There was a cool recklessness in his face, a certain keenness in his eyes that betrayed him as a man accustomed to danger. With long, easy strides he crossed the room, and Katherine noticed that beneath his cloak the silver scabbard of his Toledo walking sword slapped his thigh.

Katherine remembered herself and burst once more into tears.

"Sir? Katherine? What is going on?" When neither father nor daughter answered, Stephen directed his questioning to Katherine. "Why are you crying?"

Katherine did not reply. Her bosom heaved against its prison of whalebone so that she could hardly breathe. After taking in a great gulp of air, she commenced sobbing once more, covering her face with her fingers and weeping more bitterly than before.

Stephen pulled her into his arms and gently stroked the coppery tresses that tumbled to her shoulders in heavy waves. "There, there," he murmured gently, as if he were an older brother soothing a younger sister. "It can't be as bad as all that." He led the weeping girl to a sofa and told her to sit down for a bit and calm herself. Then, with Katherine still crying softly in the background, Stephen faced Sir Cranston.

"What have you done to her?"

Furtively Katherine peeked over her fingertips and saw her father's frost-colored eyebrows slant upward imperiously. The black eyes beneath them were cold. "Me? Surely you can't blame me for these teen-age dramatics?"

"I do!"

Sir Cranston took one menacing step toward the younger man. "Sir, have you forgotten that you are enjoying my hospitality?" His right hand rested on the hilt of his sword.

"No, but in spite of that I cannot ignore the fact that Katherine is so hysterical she can't speak. I would like to know why."

Katherine sniffled loudly. Each man stared hard at the other, as if he were an adversary instead of a kinsman. After what seemed a lengthy interval of silence, Sir Cranston smiled. Katherine was reminded once more of her father's strange habit of deferring to Stephen. He always acted as though Stephen was a man of great importance, someone he must strive to impress.

Sir Cranston said almost calmly, "I have only done what any father in my position would do. I have found a husband for my daughter. And she, ungrateful wench, repays me with insults, tears, and outright defiance!" Katherine's sobs grew louder with each word her father spoke. "Oh, shut up!" Sir Cranston's voice cracked with rage as he glared at her. "Daughter, you'll see! Your tears will not move me. I'm determined in this! You will marry Robert Morley!"

Softly, as if he desired to keep Katherine from hearing what he was about to say, Stephen said, "Sir, do you really think it wise to turn her against this man you propose she marry?"

Katherine quieted her weeping in order to better hear Stephen.

"And how have I turned her against him? I've told her nothing but good about the man," Sir Cranston retorted.

"You turn her against him by insisting so vehemently that she marry him! You know Katherine is stubborn by nature."

"I am not stubborn!" Katherine wailed.

"And argumentative, also," Stephen continued blandly, still in his softest voice.

"I am not," Katherine cried. She sat up, her eyes blazing, her tears forgotten.

"Ah," Stephen said, "I see you've regained your

tongue and dammed your flood of tears. Now, perhaps, you can tell me your side of the story."

"Why should I tell you anything? You, with your insults, calling me stubborn and argumentative. Why you're . . . you're just as bad as Father! You should apologize to me!"

"I told you once, it is not my habit to apologize, and especially when all I did was speak the truth."

Katherine rose from the sofa, and Sir Cranston, observing his daughter closely, noted the effect Stephen was having on her. The color had heightened in her cheeks, the line of her lips had grown soft, and her amber eyes glowed with animation. She seemed to sparkle every time she looked at the man. Sir Cranston's rancor evaporated. He noted the worsening of the weather, and remembered suddenly a matter of estate business which needed his attention.

"I will leave you two together," Sir Cranston said, excusing himself. They scarcely noticed his departure.

"And so, as always, you add to my troubles by insulting me," Katherine said, pouting.

"I only did so to make you stop crying."

"What do you mean?"

"You were enjoying your hysterics rather a bit too much. You'd made your point, defied your father, driven him crazy with your tears. I thought you were overdoing it a bit, so I said something to bring you up short, to get your attention. Insulting you was better than slapping you across the face or turning you across my knee, wasn't it?"

"Surely you wouldn't have slapped me?"

Stephen towered over her. He smiled and said softly, "No, Katherine, I would never hit you, no matter how you might provoke me. I have other, more pleasant fantasies about you." She felt the skin of her neck prickle with warmth. He grinned broadly down at her, then tilted her chin upward with his bejeweled fingers. His eyes lingered like a caress on her lips.

At the touch of his fingers she trembled and darted quickly away. His hand fell slowly to his side. He was grinning still as he watched her, seeming to take great pleasure as her lithe figure, so enticingly cinched into her green velvet bodice, moved gracefully about the room.

"You still haven't told me what you quarreled with your father about," Stephen said. "Your father said you quarreled about Rorbert Morley and your marriage plans," Stephen prompted.

"Yes, our argument was essentially the same as the one we had the other night. Running away changed nothing. And you cannot help me. No one can."

"Perhaps I am in a position to do more about it than you can possibly imagine."

"What do you mean?" Katherine asked, suddenly interested. She stared into his unreadable eyes, wondering if he was making some sort of joke, but he did not seem to be.

"Trust me," he said quietly.

His face remained a dark blank as he crossed the room to join her. Once more his very nearness made her slightly breathless.

"Do you know how ridiculous you look in that pompous attire," she mocked, hoping he would not notice how his nearness affected her. She tossed her head airily and firelight shimmered in the rippling masses of her hair. She moved away from him into the recess of an oriel window that overlooked the water. Outside, the wind swept up from the sea and lashed the castle walls, while the moon, partially obscured by clouds, bathed the world beneath with silver.

Stephen was at her side at once. "And you dare to scoff at the latest Court fashion? You, a mere country maid? What do you know of London, of sophisticated tastes?"

Bristling instantly, Katherine tore her eyes from the boiling sea and jagged streaks of fire in the sky. "Oh!" she sputtered. "Country maid! I know that these sophisticated tastes, as you call them, are both garish and extravagant."

"Don't glower at me like that, Katherine, when it is I who have been insulted and not you. Garish, extravagant, you say. Suppose I told you I have a trunk full of such garments and that I gave my entire inheritance—one hundred acres of good farmland—so that I could possess such a fine wardrobe?"

"Sir, I would say that if what you just told me is God's truth, you are indeed a fool!"

"Madam, you care not how you wound a man's vanity."

"You, sir, are so conceited that a little wounding of your vanity can only do you good!"

"And you, my heartless cousin, I'm beginning to think are as straitlaced as any Puritan! I dress myself with such care—velvets, perfumes—and all to impress you, and you say I look ridiculous." Stephen's eyes started to crinkle at the corners, as if he found it difficult to suppress a smile.

"And indeed, my fine lord, you do look ridiculous," she murmured.

"My dear, high fashion is always ridiculous. This style no more than any other." Winking mischievously, he patted the spot where his hose swelled over his hips like twin balloons.

Suddenly she was laughing, and so was he.

"Stephen," she said at last, "did you really sell all your lands for your clothes?"

He saw that she was genuinely concerned. "Ever the sensible farmer's daughter, little cousin?" he mocked.

Instantly angry because she thought he was comparing her unfavorably to ladies of high fashion he had met at Court, she tried to move away. He seized her hands and pulled her to him. Something fluttered and rushed in the pit of her stomach. She had the strange sensation that she was standing on a high cliff and too suddenly looked over its edge. He was laughing down at her as she struggled in his arms.

"Katherine, you are indeed beautiful when you pretend to be angry."

"I am not pretending!"

"Are you not? Then I must compliment you so that your mood will improve. Did I ever tell you that your hair is as lustrous and bushy as a fox's tail that is racing before the hounds. That your eyes are like twin topaz set in—"

Katherine wiggled frantically to escape him. "Stephen, I do not like your similes."

"Surely, my dear, you do not expect a fop to be Shakespeare as well?"

"And who is Shakespeare?"

"Ah, for all your airs you are but a country maid."

"Must you always joke?"

"Perhaps you would prefer me to make love to you?" The light in his black eyes was brilliant.

"Stephen!" Katherine writhed in earnest, but he held her tightly. "Cannot we have a normal conversation?"

"We can try," he answered simply. He seemed to be enjoying himself immensely, and in spite of herself, Katherine felt the corners of her own lips move upward.

Beneath them, not too far out at sea, a ship like a toy phantom lurched in the high seas. A wave broke and frothed across her hull, while ragged edges of sail whipped in the wind. One of its masts snapped as if it were no more than a twig. The ship, struggling in the whirling seas, was swept ever closer toward the unlighted cliffs and the reefs that skirted them. But Katherine and Stephen did not notice. They had eyes only for each other.

Chapter 7

Outside the castle a storm raged, but Katherine was aware only of Stephen—of his dark eyes gazing down at her, of his hands holding hers lightly in his, of his voice enthralling her, fascinating her with the tale of adventure he wove. Mentally she traced the symmetry of his features, his dark brows above thickly lashed black eyes, his long, straight nose, the rugged line of his jaw, and his mouth . . . Involuntarily she remembered his kisses and her response to them. There was something so vitally alive, so compelling about him. As he talked, she felt again that the two of them belonged together, that she would never be a whole person unless he loved her. Being near him, she experienced the exquisite delight of unexpectedly finding a precious possession one has believed lost forever. The feeling was intense and inexplicable. After all, he was little more than a stranger.

In spite of the cool air seeping through the crevices of the casements, Katherine grew warm. Stephen leaned closer so that his lips hovered but a short distance from hers. He was no longer speaking, and she wondered if he was going to kiss her. Even before she knew with certainty that such was his intention, something inside her yielded. She reached upward. One of her arms circled his waist and her fingers felt the warmth of his body through the padded velvet of his doublet. Her heartbeats tumbled madly after one another. She had to suppress the urge not to kiss him before he kissed her.

At just that moment Sally Bodrugan pushed open the doors of Sir Cranston's closet and came inside on the pretext of lighting the candles. When Stephen saw Sally, he flushed guiltily and sprang instantly away. With the swiftness of a bubble popping, the magic of the moment was lost. Stephen moved closer to the window and stared fixedly outside. Annoyed at the interruption, Katherine wondered again if Stephen had special feelings for Sally, who was beautiful with her clouds of dark hair. Jealousy twisted in her breast.

Stephen frowned and leaned closer to the glass. "Katherine! Sally! Look!" He pointed excitedly at a tiny object bouncing on the waves. "Do you see it? A ship! Surely . . . it is!" He muttered a string of sailor's oaths, and then, becoming aware of Katherine's presence once more, apologized. "And look . . . on the cliff!"

The Queen's Light had gone out, and crawling slowly atop the cliff, bobbing like the stern light of a ship at sea, was a light that should not have been there. Katherine stifled her cry of horror with the palm of her hand. Sally ran to another window that commanded a better view of the cliff. Lightning crackled.

"Why . . . why, it be a horse with a lantern fastened to his neck and his head tied close to his forefoot.

Someone be driving him. He do look very like a ship moving on the waves."

"Wreckers! The bloody bastards!" Stephen turned angrily to Katherine. "Tonight, my dear, perhaps we will discover which of you Cornish is responsible for these tricks!" His eyes were blazing and his words stung her, but she dared not speak as he raced from the room.

Katherine stared out the window at the desperate scene below. Mistakenly assuming that the moving light on the cliff was another ship on the open sea, the men on the storm-tossed vessel allowed their ship to drift dangerously toward the reef. Katherine chewed a nail with vengeance, and then slammed her fist against the window sill. She felt so helpless! In another instant the ship toppled drunkenly onto the rocks. A wave exploded and foamed across her bow. The light on the cliff above suddenly went out.

Far above the castle the clouds thinned into streaming wisps, allowing the moon to shine upon the world below. Katherine could see dotlike creatures racing along the gleaming strip of sand beneath the cliffs. Wreckers! For a moment Katherine despised herself for being Cornish, for sharing any kinship, however remote, with men who could perpetrate such a crime. She understood Stephen's wrath. "But I'm not like that," she murmured out loud. "I'm not and neither is my father."

As she thought of her father, she shivered. Where was he? She believed him innocent, but doubts assailed her. He had once been a sailor and knew how vulnerable ships were, how easily they could be duped with false lights. At home he believed himself invincible, the lord who made the law rather than obeyed it. Her father had sent his faithful servant Watty, who was as fierce and lawless as himself, to light The Queen's Light. Watty would do anything Sir Cranstan commanded. Had he deliberately failed to light the lamp?

Katherine's father had made a fortune from the sea and now he was marrying her to Robert Morley to gain connections with the Morleys' vast wealth. Where did such a man draw the line in his quest for even greater fortune? She remembered how he glared down at her while she wept, his eyes cold, his lips thinned with determination. She would not fool herself. He was heartless and would do anything to achieve his goals.

She remembered the stories he told of his adventures at sea, stories filled with butchery and gore. But Sir Cranston had also erected The Queen's Light, and as a result countless wrecks had been avoided. Only recently had the light failed. Was her father suddenly in need of money? Did he have debts, expenses of which she knew nothing? Running an estate of such mammoth proportions was costly. But he received rents from the tenants as well as interest from his investments in London. He owned ships. And he expected his daughter soon to marry into one of the wealthiest families in all England. Could he possibly need *more* money? On the surface he appeared to be very rich, but when a man was truly greedy, no amount of wealth was ever enough.

Katherine cast a look down at the stranded vessel. She couldn't bear to think of it any longer. She crossed the room to the empty corridor outside. Long shadows leapt upon the walls beside candles flickering in their sconces. As she hurried down the hallway, her tangled petticoats hampered her movement. She picked up her skirts and ran the rest of the way to her room.

Katherine scurried about her room, one moment frantically tugging at the laces of her bodice, the next searching through her trunk for the suit of clothes she'd stolen from Richard and never returned. She untied the strings that secured her farthingale to her waist and let it, along with all her petticoats and her velvet overskirt, fall into a heap in the middle of the floor. She could almost hear Jesse's gentle scoldings. Katherine retrieved the clothes and threw them onto the bed. She pulled the bed curtains together so that the room appeared tidy. Then she slipped into Richard's clothes and rushed from the chamber, out onto the landing, and down the staircase. When she reached the next-to-the-last step, she paused and rested the palm of her hand lightly on the carved wood of the newel post.

Before her stretched the hall, vast and empty. The only light in the room came from the faintly glowing embers of the dying fires. Chairs that should have rested beneath the great tables littered the room. As Katherine's gaze drifted upward, she noted the eerie illumination of the Cranston coat of arms. Symbolizing the Cranston might, seven deadly griffins glittered darkly as they devoured two serpents. Katherine remembered her father and her doubts tore at her heart.

"It can't be true! I won't . . . I don't believe it!" she whispered. She gripped the newel post more tightly. "I don't!" she cried out.

As if to rebuke her fervent protestation, a man's laughter bellowed from the depths of the kitchen and resounded into the empty hall. Again the man laughed, and Katherine, her hand slipping slowly from the post as she descended the last stair and started across the hall, realized uneasily that Otto Bodrugan had returned. Surely there was no one else in all the world who laughed like that. In spite of her overwhelming desire to know what was happening outside, she walked instead toward the kitchen. She had to know for sure if Otto had come back.

A balmy warmth poured from the kitchen, rich with the redolent odors of sizzling sausages, baking pastries, and fresh loaves of bread set out to cool. Because of the wreck, no one in the castle had supped. Katherine's stomach growled, and she realized that she had eaten nothing since the midday meal. Upon entering the kitchen, dimly lit with cheap rush candles, Katherine saw trenchers heaped with mutton, pies, beef, and ham. On another table perched a mountain of gingerbread and marchpane.

Hanging like a gigantic bat between two chairs was a man's rich cloak spread out to dry. Otto sprang from a chair before the roaring fire and grabbed Mary Tredeny by her apron strings. The tankard of ale he held in one hand sloshed onto the plump girl's skirts as he pulled her onto his lap.

"Otto, you be soaking from the rain. Let me be!" Mary shrieked delightedly.

Two scullery maids, elbow-deep in pastry dough,

paused at their tasks and giggled. Jesse swiftly pinched the two of them.

"What ye be ogling at, when ye've pies to make," Jesse scolded. To Otto she said, "Leave her be!" Otto released Mary, and Jesse boxed his ears. "Don't ye be looking for more trouble with the maids, Otto." She eyed her son with affectionate misgivings as he guffawed. "What's to become of ye, if ye continue in your ways?" she continued. She never ceased trying to reform her errant son.

Otto's laughter, sounding like the hollow belching of a great furnace, filled the room. Suddenly he saw Katherine silhouetted in the darkened doorway, and his chair groaned as he shifted his great weight backward. He cocked his chair on its two back legs and raked his eyes over her figure with his usual lewd appreciation.

"My great Lady Kate," he sneered, staring at her breeches. "Why you do be blest with the best pair of legs in the country! And I be the man to know." Again his thick lips parted and he laughed.

Jesse swatted him roughly with a kitchen rag. "Otto, ye'll be wise to remember who ye be speaking to," she said.

Katherine's eyes sparked as she stared angrily at Otto. There was no one she despised as much as him. If only half the stories she had heard about him were true, he was little short of a monster. Gossip laid half the bastards in the village at his doorstep. Oh, he was despicable! She could think of no redeeming quality about him other than the fact that he had Jesse for a mother and Sally for a sister. How had Jesse spawned such a . . . a miscreant?

Jesse herself was comely even though she was nearly forty years old. Tonight her wool gown was impeccable, her apron crisp with starch. She was lively and could be gay when she wasn't working. But she worked almost all the time and because she did, meals were delicious and always served punctually at the exact stroke of the hour. The castle was kept orderly and the servants organized. Yes, because of Jesse Castle Cranston was a comfortable and pleasant place to live. Small wonder that her father, who was a perfectionist in everything, had been content without a wife for so many years.

As Katherine stared at Otto's lolling form, her anger intensified. Every other able-bodied man was out in the storm trying to save that ship's crew, while Otto sat—warm and snug—in front of the hearth.

Katherine's gaze took in every detail of his appearance. He was disheveled and filthy as always. His fine clothes were soaked through. Why was someone of his lowly station sporting velvet and satin anyway? She remembered that he enjoyed Sir Cranston's favor, that there were those who believed him to be Sir Cranston's illegitimate son. Had her father given Otto his velvet doublet and embroidered undershirt? A shirt like that could cost an amazing sum. Had Otto committed highway robbery while he had been away?

Otto—her half brother? Never! She would never believe it. Katherine's lips curled faintly with contempt as she viewed him. His shaggy tangle of dark hair, his coarse beard, his prominent, red-rimmed eyes, his puffy lips—all were the features of a man who enjoyed carnal excesses. His short but powerfully built body was stuffed into garments that were too tight for him.

Otto turned his attention once more to the trencher of squab pie he had temporarily abandoned. Katherine knew squab pie was her father's favorite dish. Otto gulped it in great mouthfuls, and, with disgust, she watched liquid dribble from his lips down his neck to his limp ruff. Her gaze drifted downward to the spot where his black-haired belly peeped from the gaping space between his tightly fitting jacket and laced trunk hose.

"You eat like an animal," Katherine said at last. "Look at the floor—crumbs, a bit of sausage, a great puddle from your clothes, mud from your boots."

Annoyed by her criticism, Otto spat contemptuously over his shoulder into the fire, and the flames hissed. He rose from his chair and took a step toward her.

"Otto, will ye give me a hand and turn these chickens on the spit?" Jesse called, stepping between Katherine and her son. There was a long, tense moment before Otto turned to do as his mother had bid him. When Jesse assured herself Otto was indeed busy with the chickens, she and the maids quit the kitchen to prepare the hall for the meal that would be served when everyone returned. Katherine moved into the kitchen and plucked a piece of gingerbread off a tray. She nibbled daintily.

"I was in the hall, Otto, and I heard you laughing. I wanted to see if it was really you. After you left, there were those who said a girl from the village walked into the sea and drowned. They say she was . . . carrying your child and that you'd left because—"

Otto whirled around. "What you heard be a pack of lies!"

"Still, I did hear it," Katherine taunted. The ginger-bread was tangy, delicious.

Otto spanned the distance that separated them and seized one of her wrists. "I don't be caring who you be, my Lady Kate! You be wise not to mention that girl to me again!"

"I can see you're brokenhearted." His grip tightened, and for a moment she thought he would strike her. "Take your filthy hands off me, Otto Bodrugan!"

He released her and she fell backward.

"These filthy hands be the hands of your very own—"

"No!" she cried, refusing to accept his insinuation.

"It be the truth."

"You have no proof."

"I have eyes in me head to see that we do resemble. Our coloring be the same."

"Nothing about you is like us," Katherine said, grimacing. "You are crude . . . lewd . . ."

"I be poor, and it be your fault. If it weren't for you, *our* father be naming me his own by now and giving me what rightfully be mine all along."

"And what is that?"

"Some land to call me own. Or he could fit me with a ship. I be smart enough to know that no grand lord leaves everything to his bastard."

"At least you've some sense. But my father will leave you nothing. You're not his . . . bastard."

Otto's face was savage with anger and he would have seized her again and threatened her, but at just that moment Jesse and her maids returned. Otto was still glaring at her as Katherine said lightly, "I think I'll go out and see if I can help with the salvage work."

"It be not wise for ye to go alone, mistress," warned Jesse.

Otto laughed harshly. "With a razor for a tongue like her got, she be safe enough."

Katherine ignored his insult. "Otto Bodrugan, you are the only man not out there."

Otto sneered. "I be weary of walking four miles in a driving rain. What be it to me that fools be aground on the reef?"

"Those fools, as you call them, are *men*—men who may be dying!"

"That be the way of the world, my fine lady." Otto sat down and attacked his squab pie with one hand while the other gripped the handle of his mug. He was obviously very angry with her as well as indifferent to the sailors' fates. And he, the coward, dared to call himself her half brother!

Plunging through the iron-studded door and out into the fierce night, Katherine clutched the edges of her cloak together. Already the rain was soaking through it. A fine roan-colored stallion whinnied from beneath the sheltering cover of an eave. It looked very much like Richard's horse. As Katherine drew near the animal, she saw something heavy dangling on a coarse rope from its saddle. Hunching forward, she raced past the horse toward the cliffs. A blast of wind whipped her cloak, and she shivered with cold.

Ten minutes later the rain slackened and Katherine, breathing heavily because of her hard walk, stood on the cliff above The Jaws. Granite dived into a sea where the high winds beat the waves to a fury. Stephen

97

stood in the bow of a small lifeboat that rocked and plunged with each swell. Richard stood in the bow of another. They shouted directions to the men who manned the oars. Katherine could see the rocks—the teeth of The Jaws—gleaming like silver knife blades in the moonlight as the waves curled around them.

Knowing that the undertows near The Jaws were treacherous, Katherine cried out, "Oh, Stephen! Stephen! Be careful!" But her words were lost as a rush of air gusted upward from the sea and moaned.

She was determined to descend to the beach, but as she looked over the cliff's edge, fear took her breath away. Granite cliffs, slippery from rain and spray, plunged two hundred feet to jagged rock. Stephen was down there battling the elements in the very mouth of The Jaws. She had to be near him! She cursed her cowardice.

At last she took her cloak off and threw it onto the ground so that it wouldn't tangle in her legs and cause her to fall. She was so numb with fear, she scarcely felt the freezing rain. Taking a path she had used all her life to reach the sea, she began to climb down the cliff. She told herself that the trick was not to look down. Twice she fell, clutching desperately at gorse and granite to halt her fall. Her hands were soon raw and bleeding. Once—for two horrible seconds—her feet dangled in midair as, holding on to a clump of prickly gorse with all her might, she kicked the air helplessly before at last finding a foothold. Another time, when her foot touched what she thought was solid granite, the rock crumbled beneath her weight, a shallowly rooted shrub came loose in her hands, and, screaming for her life, she nearly fell. At last, swearing rigorously, she landed on loose sand and scampered across the beach in time to see Richard's boat lurch violently in the whirling waters, plunging Richard himself into the waves. Instantly Stephen jumped in after him. Fearful of the notorious eddies, whose dangerous currents could suck a man under and hold him there, Katherine strained to catch sight of the two men, but failed. She knew Richard was a strong swimmer. But was Stephen?

Oh, Stephen! Even now he could be drowning or lie beaten against the rocks. In a flash of self-knowledge she knew that she loved him. She had loved him from the first moment she'd set eyes on him. She would always love him, even if he never returned her love, even if she were married to Robert Morley.

One of the boats circled above the spot where the two men had disappeared. The other boat was heading for shore, and Watty was running out into the surf to meet it.

Katherine saw Clara—a lone, erect figure, her cloak blowing back from her neck like great spreading wings, her black hair, usually so neatly bundled into its netted chignon, hanging in dripping masses about her shoulders. Her face ravaged with emotion, she stared avidly into the darkness as if her heart were breaking.

Katherine ran to her, and they embraced wildly. She had never before seen Clara so frantic.

"Oh, Katherine, they're out there! Richard! And Stephen! They may be drowning!" The tones of her normally musical voice were high-pitched and shrill.

"We can only hope and wait, Clara."

"If only there was something I could do to help him!"

"*Him! Him!*" The word pulsated, repeating itself with the steady rhythm of a drumbeat in Katherine's brain. Did Clara love Stephen also? Did he return her love? Was he another such as Blake, who courted his women two—she remembered Sally—three at a time? The calm, cool Clara whom Katherine had always known was gone, and in her place stood a wild-eyed creature whose face was tormented with agony. It was obvious to Katherine that Clara loved Stephen as much as or more than she herself did. But what did that matter now, if only he could be safe? She would let Clara have him gladly, let any woman have him, if only he would live.

Hours seemed to pass instead of seconds. Katherine watched Watty jump into the boat that had returned to shore and shout his commands. The boat, tipping and tossing in the chopping surf, headed once more for The Jaws.

Suddenly Katherine saw Stephen's head break the surface of the water. A great weight seemed to be dragging him under, requiring all his strength just to stay afloat. Then she saw that Stephen had somehow managed to pull Richard's head above the water also. Richard, his yellow hair flowing in the waves, was either dead or unconscious. Watty bent over the side of the boat, secured a rope beneath Richard's armpits, and pulled him into the boat. With what looked like superhuman effort, Stephen heaved himself into the lifeboat beside Watty. Then the little boat, plunging precariously and nearly capsizing twice, headed for shore once more.

When she knew Stephen was safe, Katherine noted the conspicuous absence of her father. Where was he and where were his men? Only Watty and a few of his servants were here. Had he nearly been caught tonight trying to recover this ship's cargo? Katherine shuddered and tried to put such thoughts from her mind. She splashed into the waves to grab the bowline. The coarse hemp cut into her raw palms, and she cried out in pain. Gorse thorns were still embedded in her hands. Stephen leapt from the boat and circled her with his arms. Together they pulled the heavily laden craft into shallow water.

Above the roar of the surf, he yelled curtly, "You fool! You should not be here! This is dangerous work—men's work."

"I only wanted to help." Her relief that he was safe shone in her eyes.

"Did you think you were helping when you nearly fell from that cliff?"

He turned from her and helped Watty and the other men lift Richard's limp form from the boat. Before Stephen wrapped Richard in oilskins, Katherine saw that her cousin's shirt was stained dark with red.

"He was sucked under and caught between two rocks," Stephen said. "I thought he'd drown before I could get him out, but he's still alive. Though barely. Clara!" The Spanish girl toppled unconscious into his arms. Gently he laid her on the sand beside Richard.

Katherine watched as Stephen pressed his ear against Clara's bosom. "She's fainted."

"The strain of worrying was too much for her," Katherine said.

"We must get her and Richard to the castle," Stephen said. "Richard has lost a great deal of blood."

Richard lay on his bed. His injuries were serious, and the physician feared for his life. Jesse, cool and efficient, hovered over him, administering her potions, changing his bandages, crooning softly to him when he cried out from pain.

"Jesse be here," she soothed. "Ye be safe enough now, Master Richard. No, don't ye be moving."

Clara stood in a darkened corner of the sickroom, ashen-faced, still dripping wet and shivering, but determined not to leave.

In the winter parlor Stephen stood before the fire with Katherine at his side. As he bandaged her thorn-torn hands, he detailed the specifics of the night's adventure. He seemed more vitally alive than she had ever seen him. He thrived on danger.

"And where was my father while all that was going on?" Katherine asked slowly, trying to keep all emotion from her voice.

"He and his men were chasing the wreckers."

"You actually saw them?"

"Only from a distance. We couldn't identify them. When they saw us approaching, they scattered in all directions."

"And why was The Queen's Light out?"

"It was deliberately extinguished."

"You are sure Watty lit it?"

"Your father claims Watty is the most trustworthy servant in all of Cornwall. Watty says he lit it. If we can't believe him, whom can we believe?"

Katherine knew Watty would do anything her father commanded and could be trusted only so far as his master. And his master, her father—was he, in truth, the mastermind behind these criminals?

"Ouch," she cried. "You're pulling it too tight!"

"Sorry, love. I'm not as good a nurse as Jesse, but Richard needs her more than you do."

"Nevertheless, try to be more gentle."

He secured the last strip of bandage. She was enjoying his presence, and didn't want him to leave.

"And everyone on the ship was lost?" she asked, hoping to prolong their conversation.

"Yes, but I think we will be able to recover some of her cargo."

"When I saw you go under the waves, I thought you'd drowned."

He stared deeply into her eyes, and she looked away. Always when he looked at her like that, she thought he was reading her mind, her soul, her heart. Whatever happened, he must never know how she loved him. He cared no more for her than he did for any other woman. She was no more than a conquest to him, and if he discovered that she loved him, he would only use this knowledge to suit his own purposes of seduction.

He poked savagely at the fire and a great log fell, showering them with sparks. Stephen pulled her away. As he brushed her breeches to rid them of any flaming material, she trembled with the strange excitement she always felt at his touch. Now, realizing that she loved him, her feelings were more exquisitely intense. Sensing her response, he slowed the brushing action of his hands so that he was almost stroking her legs. She tried to pull away from him.

"Sir . . ." She tried to make her quivering voice sound indignant. "You seize every opportunity to behave as scandalously as possible. Take your hands off me!"

"A man would be a fool not to take advantage of his opportunities. You are very lovely, Katherine." Again he stared deeply into her eyes. "Has anyone ever told you that you have the most beautiful legs . . ."

"As a matter of fact . . . yes!" she taunted. "Just tonight."

She was amazed when he was instantly enraged.

"Doubtless your insipid Blake." He spoke harshly, his expression dark.

"No."

"Then you have other lovers."

He was very angry. Could he be jealous? Katherine banished that idea immediately.

"No!" She tried to move away from him, but he grabbed her arm. The breadth of his shoulders was massive. His eyes glittered with passion. She thought again that it would be wise to keep such a man from growing too angry.

"Stephen, you're hurting me!" she cried out.

"Perhaps it will teach you not to speak to me of other men," he said roughly.

"You brought them up in the first place. Why should what I do matter to you anyway?"

"It matters to me more than you know. Perhaps in the very near future I will explain why."

"If what I do is so important to you, why do you chase other women?"

"Chase other women? What are you saying?"

"Sally . . . and Clara."

"Sally Bodrugan? And Clara? Are you serious?" She nodded her head. Then he, his good humor suddenly restored, threw back his head and laughed. "Why, Katherine, I do believe you're jealous."

"I'm not jealous!" she snapped. "I don't care what you do or what you say or what women you chase. It's just that Blake courted me as well as Julia."

"I am not like your stupid Blake." Once more she had angered him. "I want you, Katherine, as he never did. And one day very soon you will belong to me."

These words, rather than making her happy, chilled her, for he meant only that he intended having her for his bed partner. She choked back an angry retort. What was the use of quarreling further with him. She determined once more that she must never let him know that she loved him, for he would surely use it against her. She had been a challenge to him, but no more.

He pulled her to him so that her breasts swelled against the thick muscles of his chest. He lifted her chin and stared down at her face. "Katherine, when you were tromping out into the waves, you did seem wildly joyous I was safe. Your eyes were shining with something I'd never seen in them before. And just now, when you said I was chasing Sally and Clara . . . I wondered . . . Why, if I didn't know you for the heartless wench you are, I'd think you cared for me."

Before she could answer, he covered her lips with his. Unable to resist, she threw her arms about his neck and stood on the very tips of her toes. When at last he released her, she managed breathlessly, "I do have a certain cousinly affection for you, Stephen."

"Your kisses are too enthusiastic to be cousinly," he said. "You should save them for the man you truly love."

Eagerness, raw and bright as a greedy flame, lit the darkness of his eyes as he drew her once more into his arms.

Chapter 8

The flat surface of the becalmed sea gleamed like a giant silver platter, and Katherine, trudging in the thick sand, shielded her eyes against its glare. Two days had passed since the ship had foundered, and she wanted to view its remains. She had to step over planks and other flotsam littering the beach. She saw the ship—her masts splintered, her framework exposed like a naked rib cage—trapped among the innocent-looking pink rocks of The Jaws. Katherine hiked her woolen skirts above her ankles to clamber over an extra-large piece of driftwood, and there, directly in her path, lay the prostrate form of a man. The exposed flesh of his neck was blistered a dark purplish red. His lips were dry and cracked. His clothes smelled strongly of the sea.

As she knelt over the man, Katherine saw that he was alive. His hair was matted with a black, crumbly substance. He had received a severe blow to the head. Unbidden, the thought came to her that possibly the man had managed to swim ashore whereupon the wreckers had bludgeoned him, robbed him, and left him for dead. Perhaps others like him had met similar fates.

When Katherine returned to the castle for help, her father seemed to tense when he learned there had been a survivor. Was it because the survivor, when he recovered, would be able to reveal the identity of the wreckers? Had her father something to fear?

The man lay in a comalike condition for days. Liquids were forced down him and his color improved, but he lay in his bed unconscious and mute.

Jesse's other patient, Richard, improved daily. Clara, glowing with an unusual radiance, never left his side. One afternoon when Katherine entered Richard's chamber, Clara jumped away from his bed, and Katherine realized that the two of them had been embracing.

So Clara loved Richard and not Stephen. Katherine was relieved that this was the case, and she wondered how long they had loved one another.

As the last days of April swept by in a great rush, with Jesse flying about the castle directing the servants at their chores until the castle almost sparkled in anticipation of Julia's June wedding, Katherine found little time to dwell on things that normally would have worried her. She scarcely noticed how easily Sir Cranston forgave Otto all his pranks. Nor did she ponder the possible reasons behind his leniency. She had no time to think that, although Sir Cranston never mentioned Robert Morley, he had not changed his plans about that marriage. She did, however, notice that she saw little of Stephen, and she wondered if he were avoiding her deliberately. She found herself curious once more as to the nature of his business in Cornwall. Why did he find it necessary to ride about the moors for days on end? Katherine noticed that Sally Bodrugan was also frequently absent from the castle, and she imagined that Stephen was with her. Thinking of them together, she grew listless and despondent.

Time passed, and the sailor she had found on the beach still lay unconscious.

On the last morning of April, Jesse ordered the entire household to gather a fresh supply of grasses, rushes, and wildflowers to provide a natural carpet for the stone flooring of the hall and corridors. The smaller, private rooms had been recently carpeted with rugs. This changing of the rushes in the hall was the last of the major tasks that needed to be accomplished to ready the castle for the holiday and wedding celebrations.

In anticipation of May Day, all the windows and doors were adorned with greenery. Even the poorest cottages were draped with branches of budding thorn. May Day was one of Katherine's favorite holidays. There would be the parade and the dancing beneath the Maypole in the afternoon. In the evening Sir Cranston planned a ball at the castle to announce Julia's betrothal.

Katherine was in the kitchen inspecting the steaming fruit puddings that were cooling on the window ledges. Golden sunlight streamed through the windows. Outside, the moors were aflame with colorful patches of wildflowers. Already summer was in the air, and a lazy warmth pervaded the kitchen, heavy with the velvety smells of redolent blossoms, newly turned earth, and the fresh sea air.

Humming merrily to herself, Katherine leaned on

a window ledge and stared dreamily outside. The sunlight made her feel drowsy. Suddenly Stephen was at her side, and before she could stop him, he took one of her hands in his and pressed it to his lips, as if she were a grand lady at Court. The warmth of his breath between her fingers was electric, and as always she trembled from his touch. His hair seemed midnight-black in contrast to his richly embroidered scarlet shirt. His skin was tanned from his frequent rides upon the moors. She thought she had never seen a man so handsome as he.

"Your father told me I would find you here," he said.

Katherine marveled that her father made it easy for her to be with Stephen when he had so disapproved of her relationship with Blake. Nevertheless, a mad gaiety possessed her as she realized Stephen had deliberately sought her out.

"Why don't we have a picnic on the moors—together?" he asked. His black eyes sparkled mischievously, and she found it difficult to resist their appeal.

"But Jesse . . ."

"No *buts*. Katherine, I've missed you so."

Something seemed to melt inside her. She heard a tiny voice that didn't sound at all like hers answer, "No more than I've missed you."

He pressed her hands and examined them.

"You see, I am a good nurse. Why, they've almost healed."

He kissed the reddened places where the thorns had been removed, his eyes gleaming with a strange intensity.

She musut be very, very careful when she found herself alone with him, she told herself. Now that he had not been so often with her, she found his power over her had increased.

Stephen tethered their horses while Katherine, a vivid splash of cranberry velvet sitting very near the edge of an awesome granite cliff, spread out their picnic lunch on a cream-colored quilt. A slow, secretive smile lit her face. She had deliberately selected this spot for their picnic because it was beautiful and private and, therefore, romantic. A small copse of stunted trees served a twofold purpose by hiding them from view of the castle windows and providing a shady coolness.

Still smiling, Katherine peered over the edge of the cliff. Oh, it was as breathtaking as she had remembered. A slender ribbon of white sand held in check an aquamarine sea. Rollers of silver waves slid easily across the sea's surface to gently caress the beach and then once more ripple back into the sea, leaving the sand glistening. Further out, the sea was peacock-blue with patches of undulating purple. Small boats filled with excited fishermen scrambled to rendezvous with the purple shadows, schools of pilchard. There would be a good catch today. Then her mind turned to the tall, dark man who, having finished with the horses, knelt beside her. His eyes held hers for a long moment before he sat down.

At first they ate and drank in silence—sweetmeats, cheeses, biscuits, and wine—too much wine. After a while Stephen talked, telling her of himself, his family, and Devon. She warmed to him and wished they could always pass their time so happily together.

"Gorse and granite, heather and sea. That is Cornwall," Stephen said. "Beautiful and wild." His voice softened. "Like you."

Again she had the uncanny feeling that the very air that held them apart was charged. It was the wine, she told herself, and the beautiful afternoon.

She listened breathlessly as he continued, "Your eyes are what make your face so arrestingly beautiful, my darling. The rest of your features are gentle, demure even, but your eyes are untamed, wild like the land in which you live."

He had called her darling! His hands were in her hair, loosening the pins that bound it, till it came loose. The wind caught it and blew it away from her face.

Then he was leaning over her, crushing her into a bed of thick grasses and kissing her as he had never kissed her before. His voice, low and musical, whispered endearments he had never uttered before.

"I love you, Katherine, as I've never loved any woman. And I want you . . . as I've never wanted any woman."

His kisses became urgent, demanding. Surely her blood was afire. In a dreamlike haze she felt him fumbling with the lacings of her bodice. Still, she did not stop him. Perhaps it was the wine, perhaps she sensed this might be her only chance to experience the rich delights of physical love with the only man she could ever desire. If she were married to Robert Morley, the years of her life would stretch ahead empty of all feeling. Her heart would wither, and she would grow old before her time. She felt a strange desperation—she had to live this moment fully because Stephen and the time she had with him were slipping away.

Stephen's fingertips gently pushed her gown from her shoulders. Her heart hammered madly, and a wild, leaping joy coursed through her as she waited for him to possess her. But instead he pushed her roughly away.

"You must get dressed, Katherine. At once! And brush those burrs out of your hair!" His voice was harsh.

She felt hurt, stunned, and somehow cheated.

"But why?"

"Because . . . I don't know why!" And then hoarsely, "Just do what I say—before it's too late!"

"Don't you want me?" Something caught in her voice.

"Yes, damn it, I want you. But you are important to me. I never knew how much until the night of the wreck when I looked up and saw you hanging from that cliff and I thought you'd fall. You're the loveliest and the most courageous woman in all the world. You're much too fine to be no more than a romp in the grass on a sunny afternoon when we've both drunk too much wine."

"Somehow this . . . this nobility of motive seems out of character. For weeks you've tried to seduce me and now . . . you . . . you suddenly . . . I don't understand you at all!"

"Neither, my dear, do I," he said wryly. "I assure you I've never behaved so strangely before. But I think when the wine has lost its power you will be grateful for my sudden, if uncharacteristic, nobility of motive, as you call it." He was smiling at her, his gaze tender. He plucked a twig from her hair. "I have feelings for you I don't fully understand. I want to protect you, even from myself." When he drew her once more into his arms, he was trembling with emotion. He pressed her to him tightly. "I never knew that any woman could matter to me as you do. Know this, my love, I would never intentionally do anything to hurt you."

Katherine drifted through the rest of the afternoon in a dazed, happy state. Stephen had said that he loved her, that he wanted to protect her, and she believed him.

The shadows lengthened and the sun hung above the horizon—a hot, orange ball streaking the sky with its fire and highlighting the trunks of the trees in the garden so that they gleamed like masts of reddish gold amid the soft lime-green of their new leaves. Katherine sat by the fountain in her father's enclosed garden, mindless of the passing time, and relived the afternoon she had spent in Stephen's arms. Oh, it had been so wonderful! Her lips warmed and her heart raced as she remembered his kisses. She shivered and hugged herself closely.

She was so lost in reverie that Stephen and Sir Cranston, talking quite loudly, were almost upon her before she heard them.

She was about to call to them, but something—her father speaking her name and linking it with the name Morley—startled her and she kept silent. They were so close to her, she scarcely dared breathe. She was thankful the dense foliage concealed her from their view. The crunch of footsteps on gravel paused.

Her father was saying, "Then you agree that the marriage should take place."

Stephen did not hesitate before answering. "I do. Katherine shall make a perfect wife, and because she's mature for her age, the marriage should take place at once."

"Mature, you say?" Sir Cranston chuckled knowingly. "You are a gentleman to describe her so." It seemed to Katherine that a million pins like the needles on gorse pricked her scalp. How could her own father speak of her in that way? "She's a lusty wench and overripe for marriage. I've said so many a time. But the important thing is that at last you and I are of one mind. Just think of it! The Morley fortune coupled with my own. You will not regret your decision to go along with me in this. It is obvious Katherine trusts you and regards you as a friend. I will leave it to you to convince her that this marriage is right."

There was a pounding so fierce inside Katherine's head that she could barely hear Stephen's answer.

"It won't be easy. She is set against it."

How could Stephen? How could he? her brain screamed. She could understand her father's motives, but Stephen's—what were they?

The question had scarcely formed in her mind before she learned the answer.

"Nevertheless, I leave it to you to think of a way," Sir Cranston said. "You know as well as I that a fortune hangs in the balance, and you will be richly rewarded for your efforts."

So that was why Stephen had not made love to her this afternoon! Her father was paying for his help.

Stephen had been lying when he said that he wanted to protect her—even from himself. There had been other reasons, less noble and more profitable, that explained his behavior. Her father's words were like a missing piece of a puzzle—without the piece, the puzzle made no sense, and with it, all came clear. Stephen had deliberately made himself attractive to her so he could use his power to persuade her to marry Robert Morley. He had not made love to her because he did not genuinely desire her. He was attentive to her only because he had entered into this sordid bargain with her father.

Their retreating footsteps ground into the gravel path once more. Her father was laughing loudly, sounding very pleased with himself.

Oh, she hated them! How could her father marry her to a man who had killed his first wife? How could Stephen on the very same day he had said he loved her have such a conversation with her father? And all for money! Oh, they were monsters!

Stephen! There were no words bad enough to describe him. Why did she fall in love with men who felt nothing for her? Why was she so gullible that a man had only to murmur a few sweet words and she was head over heels in love? First Blake and now . . . Had she no intelligence?

Katherine peered through the foliage and watched as the two men disappeared arm-in-arm in the direction of the stables. When she was sure they were gone, she ran stumbling from the garden. A branch snagged her flying skirts, and she heard velvet ripping as she pulled it free. Her head pounding, she reached the terrace steps, and paused to collect herself. It would never do for the servants to see her thus. She stood for a long time on the flagstones, mindless of the rapidly darkening sky with its peppering of new stars, mindless of the fresh spring scents.

Her heart was breaking. She loved Stephen, and he was helping her father marry her to Robert Morley. It was incomprehensible that he could do such a thing. But she'd heard him. She couldn't be mistaken.

Tears drenched her cheeks and made the garden swim. She shook violently as if she were buffeted by a high wind. She willed herself to stop sobbing, and when she could not, she decided she must somehow get to her room. At any moment a servant might come to the terrace and discover her.

Luck was with her; the hall was deserted. No one saw her as she entered the castle. Moments later, as she hurried down the darkened hallway to her room, she thought she noticed the door of the shipwrecked man's room move slightly, and a shadow darken momentarily the ribbon of light beneath the door.

Even in her state of near-hysteria the movement struck her as being odd. An inexplicable terror possessed her, and she hesitated before the door.

More than anything she wanted to go to her room where she could be alone. But she felt responsible for this man—perhaps because she had found him. During the weeks of his convalescence she had done everything in her power to protect him.

Now as she paused before his door, she felt he needed her as he had never needed her before. She must put her heartache aside and make sure he was all right.

The latch rattled in her shaking fingers. She opened the door and noticed at once that a strange scent lingered, a heavy male odor of horses, leather, and dried sea life. There was a draft in the room.

The thick damask draperies stirred, and she was about to cross the room and see if a window had been left open when the man on the bed groaned. She rushed forward and bent over him. His brow was cool and he was still unconscious, but she thought he looked better. Perhaps one day very soon he would regain consciousness and speak.

Finally deciding that he was all right, she went to her room and bolted herself inside. Without bothering to undress, she parted the bed curtains of her bed and threw herself across it, thinking no more of the sick man. Instead she heard Stephen's voice saying smoothly, "Because she's mature for her age, the marriage should take place at once."

"Mature! At once!"

She remembered the feel of his skillful hands slipping her gown from her shoulders, the fire of his touch. She had become shivery with desire; her heartbeats had quickened with anticipation. Oh, she had wanted him! He had known how much. And now he was using this knowledge against her. Oh, if only she could make herself hate him as much as she loved him!

Time passed but Katherine scarcely knew it. She sobbed for hours—great wracking sobs that exhausted her. She fell into an uneasy slumber and again she dreamed the nightmare that so frequently haunted her. As always, she stood before an altar gowned in white lace and ribbons, and when she turned to look at her bridegroom, his features were skeletal. He leaned over her as if intending to slip the ring on her finger, but instead he pushed her down a staircase that went on and on into the darkness. She awoke screaming, only to fall restlessly asleep once more.

Once, when she awakened, she thought she heard something rustle faintly outside her door. The latch of her door moved as if someone tried it. When she cried out—her voice a thin wail of terror—there was no answer save the faraway whisper of a footfall on the landing.

Chapter 9

A ray of light slanted into the bedroom and awakened Katherine. It was May Day. Although it was early she could already hear the servants' laughter bubbling up from the hall. Mary Tredeny pounded on her door.

Katherine, a sorry spectacle—her eyes shadowed, her hair tangled, and her cranberry gown torn and mussed—arose to let Mary in. She wondered how she would get through the day. The fierce drumming in her brain had subsided, but in its place was a dull ache. She rubbed her temples.

"My Lady Kate." Mary's double chin quivered and she placed both hands on her ample hips. "You do be a sight."

"Hush!"

Mary ignored her mistress's command. "Your gown, it be torn."

"And it will be your job to repair it," Katherine snapped. "Here, help me out of it. And bring some water. I want to bathe."

"My Lady Kate, there do be one thing I must tell you. You asked me to keep my eye on that man that were shipwrecked . . ."

Katherine felt again that feeling of inexplicable terror she'd felt last night.

"Yes. Go on."

"He be dead. Last night in his sleep."

Katherine reeled and sagged against a bedpost.

"Oh, my God! What happened?"

"Jesse found him this morning, stiff as a board and cold as a bowl of porridge when the warmth be out of it."

Katherine remembered the stealthy movement at his door the night before and her strange sense of foreboding. Trying to keep the tones of her voice even, but not fully succeeding, she asked, "Did it appear he died naturally?"

"I be the one to lay him out. There be not a mark on his body."

Katherine sat before her glass and stared unseeingly at her pale reflection. So the man was dead. Dead men didn't talk. She imagined there were those in the castle who would be all the more enthusiastic in their celebrations of the holiday. Perhaps he had died of natural causes. Still, she knew there were ways to kill a man and leave no mark. There was poison or suffocation. She shivered involuntarily.

Mary, her stout hands roughly brushing the tangles from Katherine's hair, cried out, "My Lady, you be covered with gooseflesh!"

At just that moment Julia burst into the room, raced to the windows, threw them open, and surveyed the colorful garden beneath with delight. "Praises be!" she shouted in a clear voice. "A fair day!" Then she skipped lightly about the room, singing gaily:

"It's May, it's May, the merry month of May!
So joysome, so gay. Let's frolic! Let's play!"

"Julia, have you gone mad?" Katherine asked, tiny frown lines creasing her forehead where her eyebrows moved together.

"Oh, Katherine, don't be cross. Not this morning. Today I'm Queen and your uncle is going to announce my betrothal to Blake!"

"Oh, yes. How could I be cross on the day we celebrate those two joyous events?" To Mary, Katherine added, "Help Lady Julia drape her petticoats over her farthingale. It will never do for our giddy bride to go about looking like a lopsided bell."

Julia tried to ignore Katherine's dark mood. She was so excited she could scarcely hold still while Mary arranged her skirts. Katherine thought she had never seen Julia looking more beautiful. Animation flushed her cheeks and made her eyes sparkle. Her tiny figure was laced into a gown of white linen from which blue silk petticoats peeped daringly. Her hair hung loose about her shoulders and, catching the light, gleamed like spun gold.

As Katherine looked at her radiant cousin, her girlhood companion, she put aside her own troubles. She crossed the room and embraced Julia.

"Oh, Julia, dear Julia, I am so happy for you." She hugged her fiercely.

"Katherine, darling, you're weeping."

"From joy for you, dear cousin." Her voice was thick with tears. "I do hope Blake makes you happy."

The faint strains of musical discord tinkled into the room. Julia, leading her weeping cousin by the hand to the windows, looked beyond the garden. "The

Maypole!" she cried. "Where could they have found such a large tree? Look! It's taking eighteen yoke of oxen to drag it across the rocks! And look at all the bright flowers on their horns!" She gave a little jump of excitement and her great skirts bounced. "People are leaving the castle to join the procession."

But Katherine was not listening. She was thinking that today of all days no one would mourn the sailor's death. Because of the holiday no one would even think of him. She wondered uneasily if someone had deliberately planned it that way.

Julia turned her attention once more to Katherine. "Darling, don't look so upset. You must dry your tears and get ready. The wagons are already hitched to take us to the village. And Katherine, don't worry about me. Please. I'll be very happy with Blake. I know I will. After all, he is the most wonderful man in all the world."

Julia had meant to comfort her cousin and was further distressed when Katherine seemed suddenly to be strangling between sobs.

"You'll see, darling," said Julia. "We'll be as close as we always have been—like sisters. You won't be losing me to Blake but gaining Blake as a brother. You know, darling, Blake is very fond of you."

Katherine continued to sob.

"Oh, darling. There . . ."

The Maypole, wreathed in greenery with its gaily colored streamers fluttering in the breeze, stood in the very center of the village square. The ground beneath it had been smoothed for dancing and on all sides of the dancing area stood leafy booths brightly decorated with flowers. Beneath the shade of these booths people sat or stood around long tables as they ate and drank their fill.

Normally Katherine would have exulted in the sights and sounds that bombarded her, but she could not share in the wild hilarity. She felt alienated from all these laughing people, from the clumps of mothers who watched their children play tag and hide and seek, from the young girls who squealed delightedly as some boy showed off his portable zoo of unusual pets, from the other girls, colorful as blossoms in a nosegay, as they strolled arm-in-arm calling flirtatious greetings to the young men who stood talking together in groups. A swarm of children raced past her, squealing. The town seemed to be bursting with the crowd, and an endless chattering punctuated with bursts of laughter and gay shrieks rose and fell.

Because of his great height Stephen stood apart from the milling crowd, and even though she tried not to be, Katherine was intensely aware of his presence. He stood beside her father on the steps of the special pavilion Sir Cranston ordered erected every year so that he along with several other local notables could be assured of an excellent view of the pageant. When Stephen saw her, he smiled broadly and waved for her to join him.

She ignored his invitation, and dashed away in the opposite direction. There were faces in the crowd she did not recognize: lean, swarthy men who seemed to her in her present unhappy mood to have some sinister reason for being here, men she would not like to chance upon alone in some desolate stretch of moorland.

Just as she thought of the moors, one man arrested her attention. He was leading a team of horses, one of them a roan stallion, to the meadow to be unhitched. He turned and squinted in the sunlight, his face a patchwork of tiny creases. His features were dreadfully familiar. He was one of the men—she was nearly sure of it—who had accosted her on the moors.

Her cry of dismay was lost in the noise of the crowd. She was surrounded on all sides by people—talking, laughing, shrieking people. She had the odd sensation of suffocating. She was about to panic when cymbals crashed, signaling that it was time for the procession to begin. She caught sight of the man again now talking with Richard. It couldn't be! Richard, good, kind Richard. What connection could there be between her cousin and that man?

Then, interrupting her thoughts, Blake, dressed in a grass-green tunic fringed with gold, clasped her hand tightly in his and claimed her for his partner in the procession. She was Maid Marian and he was Robin Hood.

The Lord of Misrule marched wildly in a zigzag pattern. Behind him strutted varicolored dragons and freshly painted hobbyhorses who from time to time engaged in mock battles with one another. They were followed by Robin Hood, Katherine—who was frantically trying to catch sight of Richard and the man from the moors—and Robin's merry band of men. Brightly costumed clowns darted wildly about, playing practical jokes on the marchers, while small girls clad in blue ran before the dancers strewing flowers on the ground to make a fragrant carpet of blossoms for the May Queen and her followers to tread upon. The holiday gaiety was infectious and gradually Katherine's tears subsided.

The crowd rose and cheered wildly as Julia, in her gown of blue and white covered with a mantle of spring flowers, slowly left the parade and mounted the steps of her throne. Katherine and the rest of the procession ran to the streaming ribbons of the Maypole and, taking one in each hand, they waited expectantly.

"Begin!" cried Julia, flushing as she seated herself to watch the festivities.

The viols began to whine, and round and round twirled Katherine, Blake, and their followers. To the throbbing beat of the music they whirled in and out, to and fro, round and round twining and intertwining their gaily colored banners until at last the Maypole looked like a gigantic multicolored candy cane. All eyes were fastened upon Blake and Katherine, for they made a handsome couple.

Never was Katherine more beautiful than when she danced. In spite of her sleepless night, her heartache, her worries, and the fact that Blake was her partner (the very sight of him angered her), she enjoyed herself, losing herself in the music. Her fluid movements were in perfect harmony with it.

Katherine was totally unaware of the effect she was having on two men: Blake and Stephen. Her emerald gown swirling around her lithe figure, her reddish-gold hair shining in the sunlight, and her breasts moving heavily above her narrow waist as she gasped for breath—combined into a pleasing whole and bewitched them. Blake forgot Julia and pressed Katherine tightly in his arms. At the same moment Katherine laughed because the music delighted her. Seeing them, Stephen strained his great, muscular body forward as if ready to strike.

At last the ribbons were wound, the squeal of viols fell silent, and the dancers, laughing, collapsed into one another's arms. Katherine's troubles returned to her in a flash and her gaiety vanished. She pushed against Blake, but he was too strong.

"Let me go!" she said, panting heavily.

"You are so beautiful," Blake said. His voice was thick, his brown eyes soft with emotion. "A man could forget himself . . . forget . . ."

"Forget his bride-to-be on the day of his betrothal?" she quipped.

"Easily when you are in my arms."

"Then you must release me."

"Katherine, I have never explained why I asked Julia to marry me when . . ."

"I have no interest in hearing your explanation now," she said, interrupting him coldly.

"But you don't understand."

"I *do* understand—perfectly." Her steady gaze grew as cold as her voice. "Now, will you let me go? People are staring." When he held her still she added, "What will Julia think?"

Before Blake could answer, the resonant tones of a man's voice sounded grimly behind Katherine.

"An excellent question, my dear." Stephen's mouth curled with contempt as he bowed slightly to Blake.

Blake released Katherine so quickly she almost fell. "Blake, your father is looking for you." Stephen pointed lazily in the direction of the pavilion. "Last I saw him, he was over there somewhere."

Not knowing exactly why but feeling suddenly uncomfortable, Blake bowed stiffly. "Thank you, sir." To Katherine he said, "I want to talk to you tonight at the ball."

He pressed her hand in farewell, and Katherine, suspecting a ruse on Stephen's part, was suddenly as anxious for him to stay as she had been for him to go. She did not want to be alone with Stephen.

"Blake, don't leave me," she said, desperation making her voice quiver. "Please. Your father doesn't need you. It's some sort of trick to get you away."

Blake disengaged her fingers that were tightly gripping his wrist.

"No. Father told me he'd need me after the dancing. I've got to find him now." Katherine's eyes grew huge and brimmed with tears. "Katherine, be reasonable. I'll see you tonight, I promise." Again he bowed stiffly to the now scowling Stephen, before he disappeared into the crowd.

Furious, Katherine turned on Stephen. "What do you mean by—"

Stephen interrupted her coolly. "I see you're planning an assignation with your lover." His words were oddly clipped.

"Assignation! Why, how dare you!"

"Madam, I only dare to speak the truth." He stared down at her, his teeth flashing white against his dark skin as he laughed shortly. "God, I was wrong about you," he said at last. "I thought you were so

. . . so . . . But what does it matter what I thought. Yesterday I should have taken advantage of your wanton mood. I was a fool to think of protecting you, of behaving honorably. Your kind has no honor. You're no better than a common—"

"Oh . . . Oh!" She stuttered with fury. She had spent the night weeping over this man's treachery and here he was accusing her! "You speak to me of honor after what you've done! You should choke on the word! You pretended to be my friend. You gained my trust. And for what reason? Oh, you are despicable and I hate you! I will hate you forever!"

He frowned, as if genuinely puzzled by her outburst, but before he could reply, she ran from him. Sally Bodrugan was immediately at his side, smiling coyly up at him as she handed him a tankard of ale. He circled her waist with one of his heavy arms and she giggled merrily. Katherine, turning and catching sight of the pair, winced as if a sharp blade pricked her heart.

"And you were going to hate him forever," she murmured aloud, mocking herself.

Chapter 10

Katherine was a vision in lavender silk with burnished coils crowning her head. She laughed. All evening her laughter had been shrill and too frequent. Pale shadows—tiny half-moons beneath her eyes—betrayed her to be in a state of near-collapse from exhaustion and worry. Standing at the foot of the curving staircase festooned with colorful garlands, she conversed inattentively with Richard and Clara, surveying without really seeing the magnificent spectacle before her.

She had watched the betrothal ceremony without real interest. Julia and Blake had exchanged kisses, and Sir Cranston had produced a ring of three hoops cleverly fit together. It had been taken apart and one hoop placed on Julia's finger, one on Blake's, and one on Sir Cranston's. Henceforth, neither Julia nor Blake could withdraw from their pact without deeply insulting the other's family.

While Katherine absently glanced over the hall aflame with light from hundreds of candles and blazing torches, she was keenly aware that two men, Blake and Stephen, were anxious for a private word with her. All evening she had successfully evaded them. Whenever they had approached, she had darted away from one cluster of glittering guests to another like a brilliant butterfly nervously fluttering from tree to tree. For the moment she felt safe enough from them, and she tapped her foot lightly in time to the music. Blake and Julia were laughing and talking with well-wishers beneath the musicians' gallery. As for Stephen, Katherine knew she had only to look up, and she would meet his burning gaze. He was leaning carelessly against the ornately carved railing of the landing above her like a lounging cat waiting for his prey to make a move.

The musicians ceased playing, and just as they did, Sir Cranston's laughter mingled with Otto's and resounded throughout the hall. The two of them were now joking with Stephen. When she looked up, the amusement on Stephen's dark face instantly vanished, and his eyes fastened on her features and gleamed with a frightening intensity. She looked away shaking.

She told herself the sight of Otto and her father together unnerved her. Her trembling had nothing to do with Stephen. She hadn't liked the way her father had slapped Otto heartily on the back as though he were enjoying his company immensely, as though he had a special fondness for him. Nor had it cheered her to notice for the first time that Otto's laugh, though deeper than her father's, was similar to it. From a distance the two men did resemble each other. Sir Cranston was taller, of course, and, in his black satin doublet flashing with jewels, more splendid than the disheveled Otto. But in the candlelight and from a distance, the two men looked very much alike.

"Jesse has prepared a feast fit for the Queen herself," Clara was saying. "Mountains of woodcock done to a turn, suckling pig, cakes, pudding, pies."

Katherine stared absently at the tables piled high with trenchers of food. Jesse Bodrugan and her staff of scullions and lackeys scurried back and forth from the kitchens to the hall with heavily laden trays.

Sir Cranston's laughter boomed once more. The day's feasting and drinking had put him in an unusually jovial mood. When he laughed again, Katherine glared up at him. How could he laugh so freely and fully after vowing to marry her to the highest bidder—a murderer!

"Katherine, you're not listening."

Katherine twisted. Clara, stunning in scarlet, her skin glowing golden against the white lace at her throat, her eyes shining as Richard moved closer to her, sounded faintly impatient.

"You're far away tonight, Katherine," Richard agreed.

"I'm sorry."

"We were talking about the May Day festivities and how well you danced," Clara said.

"Thank you."

"I don't know when we've had such a turnout," Richard said. "Lots of strangers at the village today. Must've been crowded because of the fair weather."

"Perhaps," Katherine agreed. "Richard, I've been meaning to ask you. Who was that man you were talking to near the horses this afternoon? The one with all the wrinkles?"

Did she only imagine that Richard's bronzed features tensed slightly at her question?

"I don't know who you mean," he said, keeping his voice even.

"Right before the procession started you were talking to a man."

"He was doing no such thing," Clara interjected too quickly.

"But I saw him!"

"You couldn't possibly. I was with Richard, and we were nowhere near the horses." Clara's voice was smooth, her gaze unwavering. She placed a hand over Richard's as if to steady his.

Katherine was about to ask Richard about the man again, when Blake joined them.

He greeted Richard and Clara and whispered into Katherine's ear, "We can slip away to the garden. No one will notice, and Julia will be busy for some time with my mother and sister."

Katherine could think of no appropriate excuse not to go with him. "How very convenient," she replied. "Clara, Richard, you will excuse me while I congratulate Blake on his forthcoming marriage?"

They answered together, "But of course." She thought they looked relieved that she was going.

Glancing furtively over his shoulder in Julia's direction, Blake hurried Katherine to the furthest edge of the garden where the music sounded only faintly in the distance. The air was cool, fresh, and rich with the scents of spring blossoms.

"I don't think anyone will find us here," Blake said anxiously. "And now you must listen to me. Let me explain."

"I told you this afternoon—"

"I know what you told me. But, Katherine, the last person in all the world I ever wanted to hurt was you. Don't you know I would have married you if your father had agreed to it. But he told me you were promised to Robert Morley."

Robert Morley! How she hated the man. She had never laid eyes on him, and yet she hated him passionately. If her father did succeed in marrying her to him, she vowed to avenge herself in a thousand little ways. Robert Morley would pay dearly for what he'd done—every day of their life together.

"What could I do?" Blake said. His eyes begged her to understand and forgive him. "Everyone in the county is afraid of your father."

"And you more so than anyone. You're a coward! How I could have ever thought I . . . I . . ."

"Please, Katherine, forgive me! You of all people should know how I felt about you. All those months. Don't you remember?"

"Yes, I remember. You made a fool of me. You—"

"I loved you! I did! I loved your fieriness, your boldness. The touch of your skin is like satin. Oh, Katherine, surely you know all this."

"And so you're marrying Julia?"

"Because your father wants it, and Julia and I—we are alike. We get along. Your father promised a grand dowry."

Money! her brain screamed. Always money. Did money matter more than love, more than happiness, more than life itself?

"This way," he continued, "by marrying Julia, I will not lose you entirely. We will be family, like brother and sister."

His words irritated rather than calmed her. She wanted to hurt him as he, her father, and—most of all—Stephen had hurt her.

She deliberately softened her voice so that its musical tones would arouse his ardor. "Do you feel as a brother to me now, Blake? Is that the way you love me, like a brother?"

In the moonlight she was very beautiful. The scent of her perfume enveloped him. She parted her lips invitingly, and he remembered the sweet taste of those lips. He leaned hungrily forward as if to kiss her, but she moved swiftly out of his reach.

"No, I . . . I still love you," he said huskily.

For one painful moment she, too, recalled the sweeter moments of their romance. Then she remembered his treachery and her heart hardened.

"Lies!" she cried, no longer bothering to speak softly, no longer caring if they were overheard. "I won't believe your lies anymore! You let my father bully you into marrying Julia while all the time you were fawning over me like a lovesick fool! And now here you are sneaking behind Julia's back the day you're promising to marry her!"

"Shh!" Blake cautioned, his eyes wide with alarm. He reached for her, but she shoved him roughly away.

"What kind of an idiot do you take me for? You think to placate me with a few pretty lies and continue our relationship where we left off."

"Katherine, you're twisting everything! I never meant—"

"Yes, you did! Did it ever occur to you I might tell Father and Julia what you've said?"

"You wouldn't! Katherine, be reasonable!"

"Reasonable! Ha! I'm tired of being made a fool!" Her voice was shrill. She was verging on hysteria.

Blake could think of no words to stop her from

abusing him further. Goaded to the limits of his patience, he pulled her into his arms and smothered her lips with his. At last the garden was silent, but their embracing figures were silhouetted sharply by the moonlight against the black sky. Somewhere near them something stirred.

When he released her, she would have slapped him had he not seized her wrist, saying wretchedly, "You did not mean those things you said. I know that. Forgive me for what I've done." Without another word, he turned and left her, vanishing into the night.

"Oh!" Katherine screamed in murderous fury. "Oh! How dare he?" She wiped her hand savagely across her lips as if to erase the memory of his kiss.

All her pent-up feelings fused and exploded. Blake had played her for a fool! Did everyone think she was simpleminded? All of this was her father's fault! If he had stayed out of her life in the first place none of this would have happened. Blake would never have betrayed her, and Stephen would, therefore, never have gained her love.

Her anger seemed to expand like an explosive gas trapped in a mine shaft. She couldn't go back to the castle like this. She felt she would explode with rage. But the longer she stayed in the garden, the more her frustration grew.

At last she picked up a large rock and hurled it into the fountain. A wave danced across the surface of the water and splashed her gown. Straining heavily, she picked up another, larger rock and heaved it, toppling her father's favorite marble statue.

She was laughing softly with hysterical glee as she tried to dislodge still another rock, when a deep voice from the darkness cried mockingly, "Please, don't! Spare us! We're right in your line of fire."

These words were followed by a girl's light laughter, sounding like tiny silver bells tinkling merrily in a gentle breeze, and a man's low, throaty chuckle of amusement.

All color drained from Katherine's face and she froze—too horrified to speak, too startled to run. The bushes rustled and from their depths emerged an enormous man shaking his foppish attire free of clinging leaves and dust.

Stephen! With him was Sally Bodrugan, her lips curling into an insolent smirk that reminded Katherine very much of Otto.

"Well, fortunately, you missed us," Stephen said lightly.

Still, Katherine did not speak. Her mind was racing. What had they witnessed? How much had they actually heard?

Stephen spoke so softly to Sally that Katherine could scarcely hear him. "My dear, you'd best return to the cottage. I'll see you later."

Never looking back, Sally, a flurry of flying petticoats, raced nimbly out of the garden onto the path that led across the moors to her home.

Stephen turned to face Katherine. She was afraid of him as she had never been afraid of anyone in her life.

The moon washed all color from his face. Only his eyes were alive, flashing like two darkly glittering coals, brilliant with hatred. He took one step menacingly toward her, and with the moonlight behind him he seemed a black giant looming out of the darkness. He moved more clumsily than usual, and when he stumbled, she realized he had been drinking heavily. She shrank against the trunk of a tree, and rough bark tore her pleated ruff and caught tendrils of her hair. He leaned forward and imprisoned her by placing his great arms on either side of her. Anger contorted and brutalized his handsome features. He seemed a savage masquerading in his elegant attire. The thick, sweet scent of elderberry wine mixing with ale and sack assailed her.

"All night I seek you out, and you run from me. Then I find you in the arms of another man—kissing him. Blake, our celebrated bridegroom. You are a wanton, Katherine, like my first wife. But never mind her. Tonight I'll teach you a lesson for toying with me." He spoke in deadly, hushed tones.

"I was not toying with you." When he did not release her, she said, "I'm tired. I want to return to the castle."

"Later. After . . ." His slurred voice deepened and grew hoarse. He bent over her as if about to kiss her, and she twisted frantically to escape him. One of his large, brown hands wrapped around her neck and pinned her to the tree. A scream bubbled in her throat, and he silenced her with his lips. She tasted blood—hers. She pounded on his chest with her free hand, but he seized it and held it so tightly she thought the bones in her fingers would crack.

It was useless to fight him. After she exhaled, with his hand gripping her neck and his chest crushing her against the tree, she could not draw another breath. Her airless lungs, trapped by a rib cage cinched in by her whalebone corset and pressed into the tree by his ironlike chest, could not expand. Her eyes grew over-large. Surely she was suffocating.

He did not notice her distress, only that after struggling furiously she was limp in his arms and it would be child's play to have his way with her.

"Tonight I will take what you would have given freely yesterday afternoon," he jeered. "You will learn you cannot play me for a fool!"

She mouthed words that made no sound. He drew out a knife, and her eyes widened with horror. Quickly, skillfully, he cut through the laces of her silk gown. "Hold still," he commanded, "or I will cut you!" His voice was ruthless. Then very carefully he cut through the laces of her corset. For one, long, terrifying moment he scraped the blade lightly against her flesh. It was cold—like ice. Suddenly she was trembling with terror, and he was laughing at her fear.

Katherine's lungs expanded, and she breathed in a great gulp of air. Then another. Stephen sheathed his knife before dragging her to the ground and crushing her beneath him. At last she found her voice.

"How could I have been so mistaken about you," she gasped.

"It was, I, dear one, who misjudged you," he said curtly.

"Only yesterday, I wanted you so." Her voice sounded weak. She had the sensation she was falling into a deep pit and could not stop herself, that all her strength was slipping away. His brutal hands were tearing at her gown, bruising her flesh, and she could do nothing to stop him. "Then I heard you talking to Father in the garden. Oh, Stephen, how could you— for money? I thought you cared for me."

She was only vaguely aware that his hands on her body were no longer rough but gentle. His voice—a pleasing sound—became a distant droning in her ears. His gaze had softened and filled with compassion. Or perhaps she only imagined the change in him. She could be sure of nothing, for she was lost in a dizzying world of darkness and terror.

This is like death, she thought. After tonight, after he does this to me, something in me will be dead forever. She surrendered to her weakness and exhaustion and sank like a drowning swimmer beneath waves of darkness that obliterated everything—all emotion, all terror, and all thought.

Chapter 11.

The impatiently crisp tones of Sir Cranston's voice resounded in the bedchamber, but to the semiconscious Katherine they were indistinct and slurred. She burrowed her head into her pillow as if to shut them out, and moaned softly. The coverings on the bed rustled with her movements. Every joint, every part of her body seemed to ache.

Her long lashes fluttered like tiny fans, and she squinted as she opened her eyes in the bright sunlight.

"Daughter, at last you're better." His words, terse and heavy, hung in the air between them.

When Katherine's eyes brought him into focus, she saw by the hard set of his mouth and his furrowed brow that he was deeply angry. His fists were balled in his lap.

Why, he's angry at Stephen for what he's done to me, she thought, and then she remembered everything: Blake's stolen kiss, Stephen's brutal passion—all came back to her in a painful rush. For once she could appreciate her father. He would avenge her.

"Oh, Father, I feel so awful." She sat up in bed, and the covers fell away, exposing her white shoulders and bosom enveloped in clouds of saffron-colored lace.

"You're strong, and you'll recover quickly enough, I'll warrant," he said coldly. "A short while ago Mary brought your tray up. You must eat your breakfast." She was surprised no sympathy warmed his voice.

"I'm not hungry."

"Then we'll talk now. I haven't the entire morning to waste lounging in bed as you seem to."

"You act as though nothing has happened to me! As though—"

"And what, pray, did happen that should concern me other than the fact that, as usual, you have made a thorough mess of things!"

"Me!" Why, he was angry at her! She was stunned. "Clearly you don't know what happened! Last night in the garden, Stephen abused me. He ripped my dress. He dragged me into the dirt. He was going to use me as he would a harlot! He . . . he . . ."

"Stephen's version of what happened is quite different from yours, Daughter. He has explained everything to my satisfaction."

"What!" Her voice vibrated shrilly.

Whatever she had expected, it was not this. She knew her father could be difficult in the extreme, but she would never have believed he would actually sanction a man, even his kinsman, trying to use her violently. She remembered again her father's strange habit of deferring to Stephen. It occurred to her suddenly that perhaps Stephen knew something damaging about Sir Cranston, that perhaps he had come to Cornwall for the express purpose of blackmailing her father. She remembered her own suspicions about her father.

"Yes, Daughter. Last night I had a long talk with

144

Stephen, and I'm satisfied that he in no way harmed you."

"But he threatened me with a knife! He cut my dress! He—"

"There's not a mark on you. You exaggerate. You had driven him to distraction as you've often done me. I can sympathize with him completely. You would be wise to learn you cannot play with men as though they were toys, Katherine. He is not some puppy like your Blake."

"Father . . . I . . . I cannot believe you're siding with him. He was going to rape me."

"The fact remains that he did not."

"He didn't?" Her father shook his head. "But he humiliated me. You should call him out. You should have him drawn and quartered."

"Do you despise him so?"

"Yes."

"For a while you seemed attracted to him. I thought you were friends."

"And you decided to use that friendship against me. I heard you in the garden. You said he would be richly rewarded for his efforts in helping you to marry me to Robert Morley, that a fortune hung in the balance."

"Indeed . . ." Sir Cranston stroked his beard thoughtfully. "So you heard us in the garden. This puts everything in a new light. That is when you turned against Stephen . . . because of what you heard . . ." His voice was no longer harsh but filled with new understanding.

"Yes."

"Suppose I told you that you misunderstood my meaning? You heard only part of our conversation."

"I wouldn't believe you. There could be no mistaking your meaning."

"Yet you are mistaken."

"I am not! And even if I was wrong then, after what he did to me last night I will hate him always! He would have raped me . . . he . . ."

"I have told you he did not harm you."

"I can't believe you're going to do nothing to him after what he has done!"

"Even if I wanted to, I could not," he said at last, wearily. "Last night after he brought you to me, he left Cornwall for good. He wants no more of us. It seems—ironically, you may think—that he is as angry with you as you are with him. He told me that he never wanted to lay eyes on you again. And, Daughter, when he told me that, I was angrier with you than I've ever been. I wanted to wring your neck, to beat you, to . . . I could understand all too well why he became so enraged with you that he temporarily lost control."

Sir Cranston continued speaking, but Katherine did not hear him. She should have been furious that he was taking Stephen's part, just as she should have been relieved that Stephen had gone. She should have wondered why her father was so angry with her for driving Stephen away. After all, they were only remotely connected. But she thought of nothing except that she had lost Stephen forever. Forever. Surely it was the cruelest word in the English language.

Stephen is gone, she thought, and after the way he treated me I should be wildly happy never to see him again. But I'm not. I can almost feel my heart cracking into pieces. Once she had felt close to

Stephen—as if she had always known him and would always know him, as if they were each separate parts of a whole. Somehow that closeness had slipped away.

Her mouth a gray line twisting her face, she sank heavily against the pillows. Stephen had left her life as abruptly as he'd had entered it. She had known he would. Soon she would be married to a stranger she could never love. She would be one of the richest ladies in the land. It was a dazzling prospect for her father to contemplate, but not for her. Doubtless, she would spend time at Court. She would have everything, and she would have nothing. She saw the years of her life stretching before her. Without Stephen, they seemed a lifetime of emptiness.

She was unaware that her father had ceased talking and that he was observing her reaction to his news with keen interest. The skin above the yellow-orange lace of her gown was as white as the sheets of her bed; no color tinted her cheeks. Had he not known her well, he would have thought her composed. But she was too still. Her hands were folded quietly on top of the mountainous covers, and her lips were pressed into a tight line. Her body was taut as she struggled for control. Her eyes, enormous amber pools glazed with pain and bright with unshed tears, betrayed her true state.

He saw a single tear spill and trace a glistening path down her cheek. He realized suddenly how she was suffering and guessed the reasons for it. Anger left him, and his expression softened into one of kindness. He arose and left her to her grief, and she was unaware that he did.

Sir Cranston secluded himself in his closet for more than an hour, and Katherine lay motionless on her bed. After a while Mary brought lunch on a tray and, thinking her mistress needed cheering, she stayed and gossiped in a lively fashion about events in the castle.

"There be good news today. Mathaw Dreyneck were found. He were not lost in the marshes as were feared." When that subject sparked no interest, she said, "Watty be on his way to the village to post a letter special for your father to Plymouth. My Lady Kate, it be a message to—"

"To the illustrious Morleys, I'm sure," Katherine said bitterly. "Father cares not that San Nicholas misused me last night. Nothing matters except selling me like another of his properties for the highest price." She pushed away the tray Mary had brought, so that it rested beside her untouched breakfast tray. The steaming broth, the butter biscuits—nothing tempted her.

"You must eat, my lady."

"I have no will to eat—or to live, for that matter."

"My lady! Your father be arranging an honorable marriage for you with a noble lord and you be carrying on like he were selling you to the devil!"

"It amounts to the same thing," Katherine said, smiling ruefully. "And you have put it most aptly. Robert Morley is the devil."

"You be in need of a husband, my lady, same as I be." Mary crossed her plump arms above the bib of her apron and smiled dreamily.

Katherine's brows knitted together. Mary always wore that silly expression when she thought of Otto.

"I have been meaning to mention to you, Mary," said Katherine, "that you should stay away from Otto. Now don't look at me like I don't know what I'm talking about. You were thinking of him just now. I've seen you sneaking out to meet him. Don't you know what that'll lead to—a brat with no name, or worse, you disappearing brokenhearted into the sea because he's deserted you."

"Otto be not the monster you make him out to be!"

"I'm sure we don't know half of what he has done."

"This time Otto be serious, my lady. He did give me a ring to prove it." She thrust her hand before Katherine proudly.

Katherine stared in amazement at the ring Mary wore. Emeralds glimmered among rubies. It was a fine ring—too fine for Otto to afford. Uneasily she remembered how lavishly he dressed of late. He had recently acquired a good horse too. Had her father decided that if he would not claim Otto as his son, he would give him handsome gifts to show his favor? As always, the suspicion that Otto might be her half brother infuriated Katherine, and a new resentment formed: Her father was anxious to treat everyone well except her. He had taken great pains to be kind to Stephen and now he was doing the same for Otto.

"And what have you done to earn that ring, you little fool?" Katherine demanded. "Don't you know he'll tire of you soon enough? Have you so quickly forgotten Nessie and how she drowned herself in the sea because of Otto?"

Tears splashed down Mary's cheeks. "Otto be good to me, Mistress! He be good!" She wiped at her tears, her voice quavering with doubt. She backed toward the door as if wanting to escape Katherine and her accusations.

"Aren't men always ardent in the beginning phases of a courtship? He'll change, mark my words."

"Je . . . Jesse be wanting me in the kitchen, my lady," Mary stammered. Then she was gone, and Katherine was left alone with her thoughts.

"And I am no wiser than you, dear Mary," she said aloud. "For I gave my heart to a man who used me and despised me just as Otto will use you and despise you."

As the days passed, Katherine sank into a deep depression and caught a fever. A physician was called. He decreed her melancholic, owing to an imbalance in the humors of her body.

"I believe her melancholy was brought on by a poor diet," the physician declared. "In the future she must avoid pears, apples, peaches, milk, cheeses, salted meats, venison, hare, beef, goat, all fowl, fish bred in standing waters, peas, beans, dark bread, black wines, cider—"

"Stop!" Sir Cranston roared. "What, pray, in the name of heaven *is* she to eat? Surely that list is shorter!"

More physicians were summoned. They consulted their astronomical charts and studied the phases of the moon. When the moon was full, they bled her and concocted a posset of wormwood, white wine, and sheep's trittles, which she was forced—although she gagged on every draught—to drink.

Still Katherine burned with fever. At last the

physicians decreed her hair must be shorn to within an inch of her scalp to rid her of her temperature.

"Nay, she'll look as ugly as a plucked goose," Sir Cranston thundered. "Nothing else you've done has helped. How will cutting her hair help?" When their sage answers could not satisfy him, he turned to Jesse.

"My lord, I know I be not a learned physician," Jesse began, "but I think I can save her. Ye remember I did bring Daavi Dreyneck through his fever?"

"You are a miracle worker, Jesse," he said fondly. "I leave Katherine in your hands." Throwing a hard look at the cowering physicians, he continued, "And I'll warrant there are no better hands in all of Cornwall. I'll not have my daughter drinking any more of your evil-smelling remedies. They are so foul they would make a well man sick. I ask you, men, what is in sheep's dung that can heal a fever?" To Jesse he added, "May God be with you. I'll pray the night through in the chapel. With God's help and yours, perhaps she has a chance."

"She be as hot as a kettle on the hearth," Mary cried out.

When the physicians had gone, Jesse said coolly, "Remove those covers, her clothes, everything. Burn them. Bring towels, cold water. We'll wrap her in cold, damp sheets. We'll make her drink some cool tea with special herbs."

"But the physicians said her were not to eat or drink, that her humors—"

"Do as I say. Remember, I did bring Daavi Dreyneck round."

While Jesse tended Katherine, Sir Cranston bar-

151

gained with the Lord in chapel and promised to donate five times what he had donated to the needy the year before, if only his daughter lived.

Delirious, Katherine dreamed she had fallen into a pit of flame. Over and over she called to Stephen to save her before she burned alive, but he did not come.

For two days and two nights, Jesse stayed with her patient. Katherine lay as still as death. Occasionally her lips moved as if she tried to call someone by name, but Jesse could not understand who she wanted. At last perspiration beaded on Katherine's forehead; she tossed uneasily.

"Praises be," Jesse murmured as she mopped the girl's brow. "Bring Sir Cranston," she told Mary. "Tell him his daughter will recover. The crisis be past."

"Stephen . . . Stephen . . ." Katherine mumbled.

"He be gone this fortnight past, my lady, but don't ye be fretting none. Ye haven't the strength."

Katherine recovered slowly. Her father said she was as skinny as a stick, but he seemed happy that she was improving. He made no mention of Stephen's departure or her marriage, for he did not wish to upset her. She heard him tell Jesse one day that the fever had been caused because she was brokenhearted that Stephen had gone. There was something in his voice that made her think he knew she loved Stephen, and that he approved. As always, his approval of Stephen seemed strange.

Katherine knew that Sir Cranston received letters from Plymouth once or twice a week, and she presumed that he was making the necessary arrangements for her wedding. Sir Cranston treated the ambassadors of this correspondence with great deference. Their mules were stabled with his best horses and the men themselves were housed in elaborately appointed guest rooms. Doubtless when her father thought her well enough to stand the news, he would tell her of his plans for her marriage. She would have to comply with his wishes. She had no strength left to fight him. If Stephen were gone, what did it matter who she married? Her fever had left her listless, and no one could interest her in anything.

Finally, desperate to cheer her because he feared her mood would make her grow ill again, her father took her with him for a short trip to Penzance.

"The change might do you some good—can't do any harm," he thundered when she told him she didn't want to go. "We'll take Clara and Julia as well."

It was still early when they rode into Penzance, but the town already bustled with activity. In spite of herself Katherine found the liveliness of the quay irresistibly fascinating. Reining her horse away from a heap of refuse littering the cobblestones of the narrow street, she saw a warlike galleass moored in the bay. Mahogany-colored dockmen were loading the vessel with provisions—hogsheads of salted meats and sacks of meal. Further out, a stately galleon strained gently at her anchor line and moved atop threads of mist as if she were slumbering lightly on a feather mattress. Several sailors approached Katherine and leered at her, their eyes brazenly assessing her charms.

Flushing, she twisted in her saddle and looked

away from the seamen. When she did, her gaze chanced upon a man who was several hundred yards away. He stood in the shadows beneath the eave of a two-story house talking to a woman. The slope of his broad shoulders, the darkness of his hair, his easy grace, his too-elegant clothes—all were achingly familiar.

Suddenly the man turned and stared hard at Katherine. It was Stephen! Quickly moving deeper into the shadows, he said something hurriedly to the woman before vanishing down an alley. His retreating form was curiously agile for so large a man. But she noted something else—he was limping slightly, as if he'd been injured. Katherine strained forward and called to him, but the sound of her voice mingled with a street vendor's harping cry and was lost. The girl Stephen had been talking to stepped into the sunlight and furtively adjusted her shawl so that it covered her black hair.

Katherine's heart thudded wildly. A gust of air caught the girl's shawl, sweeping it back from her face, and Katherine recognized the beautiful features of Sally Bodrugan, before Sally disappeared into the crowd.

It *had* been Stephen, but what did it mean? Had Stephen only told her father he was returning to Devon? Had he really been in Penzance all this time? She remembered suddenly that Stephen had had reasons for coming to Cornwall that had nothing to do with her. There was the matter of his mysterious business, his strange rides upon the moors. Because she did not know the nature of his business and because he had lied to her father when he said he was leaving Cornwall, Stephen's presence in Penzance took on sinister overtones. Surely he would not have been so secretive, nor would he have lied to her father, if his business were honest.

Was he, and not her father, the leader of the wreckers? He had always pretended to be appalled that anyone would deliberately try to wreck ships. But if Stephen lied about one thing, could he not lie about another?

He was obviously a convincing actor. She had been so sure he loved her that afternoon when he had refused to make love to her. He had trembled with emotion when he drew her into his arms. He had held her tightly, as if he never wanted to let her go.

He was an expert liar—that was clear—and he could be violent, even with a woman. She remembered how he cut her gown away with a knife. Was not such a man capable of anything? Was wrecking his real reason for coming to Cornwall? Had he insisted on staying in the Bodrugan cottage because of its proximity to The Queen's Light? The man who controlled that light controlled the savage coastline beneath it as well.

The smells of the fish market were heavy now, and a beggar, jostled by the thick crowd, fell against Katherine's knee. She spurred her horse onward without noticing. The rest of the day passed as if a dream. Her father left the girls in Watty's care for several hours while he transacted his business, and Katherine went through the motions of shopping, of laughing with the girls over new purchases, of delighting at Mrs. Treynwal's delicate laces.

She did not realize that a strange animation tinted

her cheeks for the first time in weeks, or that her father, when he joined her for tea, was jubilant, happier than he had been since Stephen's abrupt departure. He looked as he often did when he had bested someone in a horse trade.

Julia had not finished shopping for her trousseau, so she, Clara, and Watty left Katherine and her father to enjoy tea alone. They sat in a private room in Sir Cranston's favorite inn at a table with a view of the bay. As Sir Cranston watched his daughter, a speculative gleam lit his eyes, but Katherine did not notice. She was watching with mild interest as a dainty caravel, her sails filling, plowed through the waters as she set off for some exotic destination.

"You see, Daughter, I was right. A change of scene has done wonders for you."

"Has it?" she replied absently. She turned to face him, and became aware for the first time of the calculating light in his eyes.

"I think you're well enough for some news I've recently received." He seemed strangely excited.

"Yes . . ." she said apprehensively.

"About your marriage to Robert Morley. The contract has been drawn up, the dowry agreed upon, and the wedding date set."

"Oh!" Too much was happening too fast. She had seen Stephen again, and all the old feelings—her love and her doubts—were back stronger than ever. And now, too, her father had settled her marriage contract to Robert Morley.

"There is one snag in the marriage plans," he was saying. "But I can't see it as being too important.

156

Robert Morley is occupied with the Queen's business at the moment. He cannot come to Cornwall to woo you. I have tried, without luck, to persuade him. We have agreed, however, that the wedding should take place at once because we both want the affair settled as soon as possible. We'll have a double ceremony—for you and Julia."

"What . . . how . . ." There was a roar, louder than waves crashing against granite, in Katherine's brain as she stammered. Her father's face blurred in a dizzying whirl.

"By proxy of course," Sir Cranston continued blandly, taking no notice of her horrified stare. "He's sending his sword for you to kiss, and one of his nephews will stand in his place."

"Father, I can't believe that you're really going to marry me to a man who cares so little about me that he won't even bother to come to Cornwall for the wedding. How can you?"

"The proxy marriage will be as valid as if the bridegroom were here himself." Frosty eyebrows drew together in irritation. "Girl, I don't think you realize how important the man you're marrying is. You should be proud."

"He's so important that a new bride is but an unimportant acquisition."

"You have only yourself to blame for this. You have not been overly eager to meet him. Perhaps if you had evinced any enthusiasm, he would have come. But no! You would not write any of the letters I asked you to write. I had to send him your miniature myself. And now *your* vanity is hurt. I've had enough of your defiance in this matter! The sooner the thing's settled, the better."

"Oh, you are heartless . . . heartless . . ."

"And you, Daughter, are the most ungrateful wench a man ever had the misfortune to father!"

Chapter 12

Events in Katherine's life were rapidly moving toward a climax. Robert Morley's nephew, Jason Morley, arrived with an enormous jeweled sword and was treated as if he were the grand lord his uncle was. Elaborate apartments were given Blake and his family until the wedding celebrations were over. Every night there was feasting and reveling, and in two days time the double ceremonies would take place.

Every time Katherine found herself in Jason's company she felt faintly disquieted. He was tall and slender, dark and very young. Unusually graceful, he was a marvelous dancer. There was something about him that seemed strangely familiar. She knew she had never seen him before, yet why did she feel that she had?

Katherine was no longer the pale-faced wraith she had been after her sickness. She was more beautiful than ever before, as bright with life as a candle flame that will soon be snuffed into darkness. Her movements were quick and vivacious, her laughter tinged with hysteria. Her eyes burned with a queer brilliance, as if she were possessed of high, explosive excitement. A stranger would have thought her a radiant although nervous bride, but her father observed her with growing alarm. He ordered Watty to watch her always, to follow her everywhere. He was afraid she might try to harm herself or run away again.

In this state of feverish exhilaration Katherine endured the last fitting of her wedding gown.

"Do stand still, mistress," the seamstress admonished as the silk again slipped through her fingers because of Katherine's frenetic movements. "Your cousin do be as still as a statue."

"All right, all right." Katherine twisted her hands in anxiety. She felt she was going to burst with energy. "Do try to hurry." To Julia, who stood calmly beside her in a gown exactly like hers, she said, "Cousin, how can you just stand there when these women are so slow and I'm as nervous as a cat?"

When Julia, lost in a pleasant world of daydreams, made no answer, Katherine's golden eyes darted across the room. Her gaze fell upon Clara, who was working at the loom. Clara had been staring fixedly at her, and now looked away too quickly.

Uneasily Katherine stared into the gilt-edged glass and saw without really seeing the twin reflections of herself and Julia—two shimmering angels in white silk gowns with peacock-blue stomachers tightly wrapping their waists.

Ever since she had returned from Penzance, Katherine had noticed little things that did not seem right. Clara seemed always to be watching her, yet wanted nothing else to do with her. Since the night of the May Day ball, when Katherine had questioned Richard about the man leading the horses to pasture, Clara and Richard had avoided her. They spoke in hushed tones when she approached, and if she joined them, they acted uncomfortable. They seemed to be hiding something. Were they, in some way, involved with the wreckers?

Katherine had quizzed Sally Bodrugan about the man she had been with in Penzance, but Sally had denied going to Penzance at all.

"I be here all that day, my lady. I were—'tis God's truth!" Sally, her black eyes brightly defiant, had been adamant. Katherine had wanted to shake her senseless for that lie.

"I saw you with my own eyes!" Katherine declared vehemently.

"You thought you saw her," Richard said. "I know she never left the castle because I was here. She could never have shirked her duties and gone to Penzance without my knowing it."

"And was I not riding beside you, Katherine dear," Clara cut in smoothly, "when you thought you saw Sally? Surely, had she been there, I would have seen her as well."

They were all lying. But why? Watty, Richard, Sally, and her father all seemed to be part of some plot she knew nothing about. And why did Watty follow her everywhere?

The seamstress folded the last tuck; as she pinned it, she pricked Katherine, who, starting, looked away from the mirror and saw Clara was once more staring at her. Again Clara quickly dropped her gaze, but not before Katherine saw that those great almond-shaped eyes—usually so serene—were deeply troubled.

* * *

Katherine did not want the hours to pass quickly, but they seemed to rush by all the more rapidly. On the eve of her wedding, the castle was quiet. The festivities had ended earlier than usual, because everyone wanted to retire early to be fresh for the morrow. Katherine lay shivering in the vast softness of her bed. Marriage . . . tomorrow . . . to a stranger. It was a frightening prospect that still seemed unreal.

If only she could run away again. If only there were some way she could escape. But she knew that all exits and entrances of the castle were being guarded. As an extra precaution, Watty slept on a pallet outside her door, and Mary lay on a pallet at the foot of her bed.

Suddenly, a wild desperation possessed her, intensified by her inactivity. She had to get up, to stretch her legs. Katherine slipped from her bed and pulled on a woolen wrapper. Moonlight sifted through the loosely woven draperies that floated at the windows like gossamer. As she noiselessly stepped past Mary's pallet, the sleeping girl stirred. She opened the door and stepped into the hallway. Watty, instantly alert, sat up. She pressed her finger to her lips.

"Shh, I can't sleep and I'm only going for a walk in the gallery," she said.

Watty was already shuffling to his feet, and she knew he would follow her. For once she was glad of his presence, for the hallway was filled with threatening shadows. Silvery moonlight streamed in the window at the far end of the corridor, sending a single shaft of light blazing down the swirling stairs but leaving the passage in which Katherine stood dark.

Her footsteps crackled softly as she walked upon the dried rushes in the hallway. As she glided past Sir Cranston's closet, she saw that a pale thread of light gleamed faintly beneath the closed doors. What was her father doing up at this hour? Earlier he had said he was exhausted and ready for bed. She heard the whisper of voices and became suspicious immediately. Her father's voice usually boomed when he spoke. She hesitated before the doors and strained to listen. She could scarcely believe what she heard. Her father's voice had ceased, and she heard the low and resonant tones of a man's voice answer him. Stephen! She would have known his voice anywhere. Why had he returned on the eve of her wedding?

She placed her fingertips on the brass handles and rattled them furiously. The doors were locked.

"Stephen!" she cried out. "Stephen! Open the doors!"

The doors opened almost instantly, and her father, a black giant looming in the doorway with the yellow-orange glow of the candles and dying embers of the fire behind him, seized her roughly.

"What are you doing up at this hour, Daughter?"

"Stephen . . . Stephen . . . I heard him! I want to see him!"

"Watty, for God's sakes, man, help me get this girl to her room. Didn't I tell you to guard her door?"

Together the two men dragged the furiously struggling girl down the hallway.

"I want Stephen! Do you hear me? I know he was in there!" Katherine cried.

When they at last reached her bedchamber, Sir Cranston said harshly, "Daughter, as usual, you are hysterical. You drove Stephen away nearly a month ago. You only imagined that you heard his voice. I . . . I was reading to myself aloud." He pushed her into her room and shut her in. She heard the bolt slip into place and the key turn in the lock.

Katherine threw herself against the door and pounded on it. "You're lying! Lying! I know you are!" Katherine cried.

She heard the whispering crunch of her father's retreating footsteps. He had locked her in for the night! He had lied to her! Tomorrow he was marrying her to a man who cared nothing for her, who was not even coming to claim her! Oh, her father was cruel, and she hated him!

For an hour she sat in the window seat of an oriel window and stared unhappily out onto the garden. Moonlight transformed its paths into threads of silver weaving through shadowy ornamental shrubs, crisscrossing, and forming intricate designs so that the garden resembled a Persian carpet some giant had carelessly tossed upon the moors. She saw the white light glimmering on the waves beyond. Then movement directly below caught her eyes. A tall man stepped lightly through the garden and headed for the moors, taking the path that skirted the marshes to Wellan Cove. It was Stephen! She *had* heard him! Her pulse rose in her throat as she pressed her forehead to the glass. Why had he not answered her when she had called to him? The answer was obvious: only his mysterious business had prompted his return. He no longer cared anything for her.

A cloud moved across the moon, and the scene beneath blackened. She sighed heavily and looked away.

Stephen had come back! Had he returned to save her from this marriage, as he had once promised her he would? Or had he come back only to be paid for helping Sir Cranston marry her to Robert Morley. Why did her father deny that he had returned? What secret was everyone keeping from her?

Katherine crept back into bed and a cozy warmth enveloped her. In spite of her doubts about Stephen, she felt relieved that he had come back. Her tensions ceased, and she finally slept, dreaming of her wedding day. She stood before the altar beside a tall, dark, and very handsome man who swept her into his powerful arms and kissed her. Even as she slept, she smiled.

When Katherine awoke, the sun streaked the gray sky with lavender and rose, transforming the sea into a fluid body of amethysts and rubies.

Sir Cranston unbolted her door and, stepping inside, thundered, "Well, Daughter, you seem no worse for your hysterics last night. I suppose you've grown accustomed to them."

Bed sheets rustled and Katherine rubbed her eyes. "Father?"

"I've a surprise for you that should show you the error of your ways." He thrust something heavy onto the bed that sparkled as if alive with fire. She fingered the jewels without comment. "A wedding gift from your generous bridegroom," her father explained. "You are to wear it today."

She looked up at her father, who stared intently at the diamond necklace as if he were hypnotized by it. His eyes seemed to gleam with greed.

"You should be very happy, Father," she said in a small voice. "For you have sold me for a very high price."

He tore his eyes from the necklace and examined her like a piece of horseflesh. He smiled his approval.

"You are very beautiful, Daughter, and well worth a fortune." He laughed loudly and slapped his thigh. "You may look glum all you want to, but as for me, I intend to enjoy this day, for it is the happiest day in my life. Today my daughter is marrying the wealthiest man in Devon." Almost as an afterthought, he added: "And Daughter, this marriage will make you a happy woman. I promise you."

He was moving toward the door when she stopped him.

"Father, why did Stephen come back? I know I heard him. And I saw him too—in the garden when he left last night."

He hesitated only for an instant. "Don't ask me such questions, Daughter, or I'll fear your fever has returned. I told you, he has left us, and all because of you. I was alone last night reading."

"But I *know* I heard him!"

His eyes fastened on her face with an avidity that frightened her. "You told me you despised him. Why are you suddenly so anxious that he return?"

"I . . . I . . . just want to know why you won't tell me he was here, that's all."

"Is it? I wonder. I've often said you were a lusty wench and overripe for—"

"I know well enough what you've said!" Katherine snapped. "Leave me in peace."

166

"As you wish," he said mockingly. He chuckled softly as he left the room.

All through the long morning, as her maids prepared her toilet, Katherine hoped Stephen would come to her. Only when the chapel bells began to clang furiously, only when she and a radiantly smiling Julia advanced between two long lanes of tenants and well-wishers on a path strewn with flowers—only then did she give up hope. The women bobbed low curtseys, while the men removed their caps, waving and cheering wildly. Everyone gaped at the fiery collar circling her throat. All the time Katherine scanned the crowd for Stephen. If only, if only he would come forward and save her! But she knew he would not.

Two young boys walked before the brides, holding their laces, long silk ribbons that tied their sleeves, bodices, and skirts and flowed from their gowns. Behind the girls walked an ensemble of musicians playing merrily.

Oh, it was a gay, mad scene, and if Katherine had been marrying the man she truly loved, she would have been wildly happy. As it was, she viewed the festivities with the grim enthusiasm of a condemned man approaching the block.

Clara and the other bridesmaids, dressed in saffron-colored gowns and carrying great bride cakes, followed the musicians. Blake and Jason, resplendent in jeweled white doublets and carrying magnificently wrapped bridal gifts, marched at the end of the procession.

Every face—save those of Blake and Katherine—was joyous. Katherine felt that every step led her closer to her doom, and when she turned, she saw that

Blake's eyes were also round and desperate with alarm.

No one seemed perturbed by Blake's nervousness. It seemed appropriate that the bridegroom be a little terrified. It lent an air of reality to an otherwise mad occasion.

The brides knelt before the altar, with Jason standing beside Katherine and Blake beside Julia. A hush fell upon the crowd as Katherine, choking on the word *obey*, searched the crowd one last time for Stephen. He had not come! Her lips kissed the cold blade of Sir Morley's sword. With a sinking heart she heard the dean's words as he wed her for life to a man she could never love. Numbly she watched Jason slip a wedding band of diamonds onto her finger.

Then the two brides were surrounded by a throng of young men who clambered and tugged, pulling off all the laces that fluttered from their gowns. Julia laughed merrily, and Katherine, white-faced, endured their sport.

Suddenly a tall, dark man pushed his way back through the crowd toward her. For a moment she thought he was Stephen.

But Jason, not Stephen, was smiling down at her and she, trying to hide her disappointment, smiled tremulously up at him. She scanned his features. How could she, even for an instant, have mistaken him for Stephen? This gentle, shy boy, his olive skin flushed with embarrassment as she stared up at him—why, there was nothing of Stephen in him. She had only thought so because she wanted so desperately for him to be Stephen.

Jason was obviously ill at ease playing the part of

bridegroom. "As my uncle is not here to claim his trophy," he began haltingly, "can I claim one in his place?"

"But of course," Katherine said.

Jason's cheeks brightened once more as his fumbling fingers plucked a lace from her gown and pinned it to his sleeve.

Sir Cranston handed a silver cup of spiced wine to Julia and Blake. They drank from it and passed it to Katherine and Jason. An uneasy hush fell once more upon the crowd as Katherine hesitated before sipping from it. Her father, scowling down at her, stepped forward and lifted the cup to her lips, forcing her to drink from it. When she finished, the cup was passed through the crowd. Drinking from this cup symbolized that the ceremonies had been performed and witnessed.

Katherine's fate was sealed forever. The sweet taste of the wine lingered and turned bitter in her mouth. Everyone was laughing, her father more than anyone else. She knew that his happiness was tinged with triumph. He had ruined her life, and he was happy. Oh, the injustice of being born a woman!

If only she had been a man, she could have stood against him. But no woman had any power over her personal life, and even the Queen could not marry the man she loved. Daughters were the property of their fathers until they wed, then becoming the properties of their husbands. Women were slaves of men. They could not own property of their own and were powerless to make decisions. The purpose of women was to satisfy men.

Sir Cranston's laughter became a deafening roar.

Katherine observed him resentfully as he drank his ale heartily. The crowd raced and pushed past her toward the hall where extra tables had been set up. In spite of these tables, most of the many guests and servants still had to stand. The great bride cakes were torn apart and devoured with relish. The musicians resumed their playing.

Somehow Katherine found herself in Blake's arms. Once more—as he had on May Day—he danced with her and asked her to understand and forgive him.

"Should you not be dancing with your own bride?" she asked. She was surprised that she no longer felt any anger toward him for what he had done.

"I've already done so," he replied. "Julia even suggested that I ask you."

"How convenient that you have her permission."

"Sometimes," he said, "I think you delight in being perverse."

"Perverse? Me? I think you delight in insulting me."

"Will you forgive me?" Although he smiled nervously and spoke lightly, she sensed his earnestness. When she hesitated, he continued. "I know that I've behaved a perfect heel, that you've every right to be angry. But if you could possibly find it in your generous heart to forgive me, you would make my wedding day completely happy."

The music stopped, and he led her out onto the terraces that sloped to the garden.

"Blake, I don't really think we should be alone together."

"And why not? We're family now. Cousins."

"Only through marriage."

The sinking sun made his skin glow golden, and his great brown eyes were soft and pleading like a pup's as he gazed fondly at her. Suddenly her heart warmed to him. He was, after all, an old friend, a childhood companion, and her cousin's new husband. This was his wedding day. Everything that had happened was her father's fault—not his. He had not deliberately set out to lead her on. Her father had forbidden him to continue his courtship with her, and promised him a large dowry if he wed Julia. Katherine had long known the Finnleys needed money, and Blake had always been a dutiful son. If he had forsaken her a little too easily—well, it was better not to dwell on that.

She took his hand in hers and patted it. "I do forgive you, I do. And I understand why you married Julia. I'm sorry if I have behaved unkindly to you about it in the past. It was just that I was hurt and confused."

"Of course you were. And now that you have forgiven me, may I kiss the bride?"

"Oh, men, are you all so incorrigible?"

"I'm afraid that we are." He leaned forward.

Suddenly Katherine remembered the last time Blake had kissed her, when Stephen had been spying upon them. Suppose someone were spying on them now. She and Blake were alone in one of the more secluded niches of the garden. It was no secret she had thought herself in love with him. If someone was watching them and saw Blake kiss her, might he not misinterpret the chaste, cousinly embrace for something other than it was?

I'm growing cautious in my old age, she murmured

to herself as she stared into the thick hedge. Aloud she said primly, "I don't think a kiss here so far from the others would be proper. Perhaps when we return to the castle."

"And you were always so bold," he whispered. "I hope your marriage to this Morley fellow doesn't kill your spirit." Then, ignoring her protests, he pulled her into his arms with an eagerness that was more than cousinly and kissed her firmly on the mouth.

"Blake. You're family now! Remember it!"

"I fear it will not always be easy."

When he looked properly chastened from her scolding, they talked together for a while longer. In spite of her own unhappiness, Katherine found herself enjoying the growing easiness between them. She had missed their friendship more than she had realized. They talked of old times, of Christmases they had shared, of other holidays. Then they spoke of the morrow when Jason would escort her to Devon and she would meet her bridegroom. Blake tried to reassure her that her marriage would work, that her father wanted only the best for her, that he had been thinking more of her happiness than of money. At the mention of money, she moved her hand and the diamonds of the ring flashed their cold, white fire. She fingered the heavy jewels at her throat, and nothing he could say could convince her. It was almost dark when he suggested they return to the castle.

"I think, Blake, I will stay a little longer. This is, after all, my last night in Cornwall. I need a little time to myself."

"I understand." He bowed low over her hand. Then

humbly he said, "Thank you, Katherine, for understanding."

Once he was gone, Katherine found thought impossible. She became strangely uneasy. For some reason the uncanny sensation persisted that someone was watching her—someone she could not see. She tried to rid herself of the notion. Why would anyone be watching her? She should return to the castle. She could hear the faint strains of the musicians' instruments and she knew the guests would be dancing pavanes, galliards, allemandes. Usually she danced every one of them. Her foot lightly tapped the gravel in time with the music, and she realized she was humming the familiar tune.

No! She wanted no part of gaiety, when she herself was far from gay. She moved away from the thick hedges to the furthest edge of the garden. The spot was lonely, desolate. Again she grew afraid. She told herself her fears were as senseless as a child's fears of the dark. Still, she could feel goose bumps dimpling her flesh, and she shivered.

Below her stretched the bleak moorland, with hills of rock tearing the skyline like gigantic claws. Further down, she saw cattle grazing, their careful feet wary of the soggy marsh grasses, which, although appetizing, were rooted in mire. On some nights a sea wind blew across the moors, but tonight the wind was still. There was a hushed stillness, an unnatural silence. She felt again the strange sensation that she was not alone, and suddenly she was very much afraid.

Then she heard it, a rock tumbling as if someone

trying to move silently had made a false step. Whoever or whatever had made that sound stood between her and the castle. Again a pebble rolled. Surely, it was but one of the guests who had come into the garden to enjoy the fresh air. Yet, why did he take such care to make no sound? She could not return to the castle now, for whoever was approaching blocked her path.

Katherine's heart pounded in her throat. She could not control her fear. She was running, racing toward the sea cliffs. Her whalebone corset cut into her ribs as her breath quickened into rapid gasps.

Topping the first ridge, she paused for breath. The cliffs plunged to the sea on one side, the rugged terrain of the moors torn in places by tall formations led down to the marshes. She would have preferred to avoid the marshes, but she realized it would be easy to hide in the tall grasses or behind a mound of rock— if she could only get that far.

She took a deep breath and plunged forward. Going downhill was easy, but as she neared the marshes the ground became soggier. She had to be careful— one false step and she could find herself swallowed up in some bottomless hole. She grimaced with distaste. Every indentation of her feet quickly filled with water. She despised this spongelike earth and the tangy odor of rotten vegetation.

Then she heard someone treading heavily behind her. With only a little further to go, she tried to quicken her pace. Very soon it would be easy to hide in the marsh grasses. Suddenly she tripped on the sodden hem of her wedding gown and fell forward.

She screamed, slipping and falling as the damp earth beneath her feet gave way. She was sinking, being sucked into one of the very holes she had feared. She grabbed hold of a branch but it came loose in her hands. She screamed again and again.

She had always known the marshes were dangerous, but in her terror she had been careless. Terrifying visions of muddy suffocation flitted across her mind. Suddenly a shadow fell over her and for one long moment she forgot the gurgling, sucking earth and stared up into the fiercest face she had ever seen. A giant stared down at her, his leathery skin blackened from the sun. One eye was covered by a patch; the other leered at her with satisfaction, gloating at her helpless predicament.

"Help me, please," she cried. When he only laughed, she cried, "What kind of man are you—help me!"

His laughter became a roar. He pulled a stunted tree up by the roots as if plucking a wild flower. She saw the looped ring piercing his earlobe and the kerchief covering his grizzled hair and she knew without thinking that he was a pirate.

He thrust the tree toward her to pull her from the pool. Katherine hesitated before grabbing the branches. She looked into the dark water that circled her waist. Perhaps it would be better to drown than be saved by this barbarian. He watched her as if understanding her thoughts; his laughter had died to a throaty chuckle.

"Aye, take it, miss, before it be too late for me to save ye. The more ye be sucked under, the harder it be to pull ye out."

She was surprised that he spoke English, for she thought he was a pirate from some foreign land. Spanish pirates still marauded, descending in the dead of night to plunder and steal, to burn down villages and townships, to take women for their pleasure. Was he an English pirate? Was she to be another of his victims?

Despite the dangers, it was in her nature to survive, to prefer life—even the life of a pirate's mistress—over death. She grabbed the branches and held tightly as he tugged, grunting and panting, finally pulling her free.

Before she could cry out, he ripped his kerchief from his hair and tied it across her mouth. She gagged on the reeking scent of an exotic hair pomade.

Was her wedding night to be consummated by rape? she wondered with anguish. She struggled wildly, but to no purpose. His an ox's strength, and hers no more than a child's. But he was not lustful. He pinioned her arms and ankles with pieces of rope, then slung her—trussed and helpless—over one shoulder, as if she were a sack of meal and he a miller on the way to market. He began trudging toward the sea.

He walked for a long time, taking a different path from the one they had followed from the garden. At last he dropped her to the ground, breathing heavily. She heard the gentle lapping of waves on rock and saw the smooth, glimmering waters of Wellan Cove. In the very center of the cove, where the water even at low tide was many fathoms deep, a dainty caravel floated gracefully upon the surface. It was exactly like the one she had seen in Penzance.

What did it mean? Was she being abducted to pleasure a crew of pirates? Her throat ached with a silent scream. Then the man once more lifted her onto his shoulder and trudged down the cliff. He lowered her onto a boat and began to row relentlessly toward the caravel. All too soon, she saw the hull of the ship rising from the water like a cliff at the sea's edge. The man bent over her, cut the ropes that bound her, and removed the gag from her mouth. He pulled her roughly to her feet and commanded her to climb the rope ladder dangling from the side of the ship. Their movements caused the small boat to rock precariously, and she had to clutch him for support.

"Why should I board your ship?" she demanded.

"Because ye must, miss. I've no wish to hurt ye."

"Then why have you brought me here trussed like a goose for the spit?"

"I were obeying orders."

"Whose orders?"

"Ye try my patience with y're questions, woman!" He put the rope ladder into her hands. "Climb!" His eye was fierce, and, trembling with fear, she began to ascend the ladder.

Hands stretched over the ship's side and pulled her onto the deck. She was surrounded by men leering appreciatively at her. They reached for her, and she shrank away without knowing whether they wanted her jewelry or her person. Their voices babbled with excitement. Then silence fell like a spell. The man who had saved her heaved himself on deck, and spoke in an authoritative voice.

"She be not for the likes of ye, but for the captain. Take her to his cabin. Bring her a tub, fresh water, clean clothes. Ye know well enough the captain have no liking for filth, even if it be covering a comely wench."

His words embarrassed her, and she remembered

her muddied gown. Two men seized her, and dragged her below, and locked her in a small oak-paneled room. Her eyes darted wildly for a way to escape. The windows were too small for her to climb through. A single candle flickered in a horn lantern. She tried the latch of the door and found it firmly locked. There was no escape. She shivered with cold and terror.

After a while two sailors returned. They set out fresh clothes, filled a tub with water, and left soap and perfume.

Katherine removed her necklace and placed it on the captain's desk. Mechanically she undressed, bathed and washed and dried her hair. She put on the lawn chemise the men had brought and the woolen wrapper. She had no desire to make herself attractive for a pirate captain, but neither did she want to stay cold and smelling of the marsh.

When she finished, the men returned to remove her soiled gown and the tub.

Alone once more, she examined the cabin. Everything was in perfect order, reminding her of her father. It was strange that a pirate captain should be so orderly. She fingered his astrolabe and cross staff, compasses and hourglasses. She perused his neatly folded charts. She opened a drawer of his desk, and to her amazement—saw a miniature of herself, the miniature her father had claimed he had sent to Robert Morley. How had it come here? A table bolted to the floor held a creamy-yellow loaf of the finest wheaten bread, an assortment of cheeses, and a flask of wine. She poured herself a glass and drank it quickly. A narrow well-polished brass railing edged the tabletop so that plates of food would not slip onto the captain's lap when he dined at sea. The bed was sumptuously made. He was obviously an orderly man with refined tastes, she decided. He must be a successful pirate. As she became familiar with his cabin, she felt less afraid. Perhaps it was the wine. She poured herself another glass.

Her eyes drifted once more to the bed, which dwarfed all the other furnishings of the room and was piled high with thick coverings. In spite of her woolen wrapper, Katherine was still cold. The wedding day had been an ordeal, her abduction terrifying. Now the wine was making her drowsy. She longed to climb onto the bed and lie down, but it was his bed. When he came, would he think her eager to be used by him? She shuddered.

An hour passed and still he did not come. Where was he? Kidnapping more women? Raping? Plundering? What of her family? Her father? Were they safe? Would they discover that she was missing and search for her? In any minute her father might arrive to rescue her.

Her eyelids drooped. She regarded the tempting softness of the bed with weakening resolve. What did it matter if she lay upon his bed? If he wanted her, he would take her, and she would not be able to stop him. She was too exhausted to think of it any longer, too exhausted even to be afraid. She fell upon the bed and, pulling a blanket over herself, was immediately asleep.

Hours passed, and still she slept. She was not aware that someone gently picked her up, and pulling back the coverlets, placed her upon the sheets and tucked the covers about her.

When she awakened, she was at once aware of the difference in the ship. It was moving, dipping into the trough of a swell and climbing out of it once more. She heard the faint groaning of the hull, the sound of water rushing past. Just outside the cabin door she heard the heavy tread of a man's boots as he descended the stairs. He whistled a merry tune as if he was very happy, as if he relished the thought that a woman waited in his cabin to pleasure him.

Her breath caught in her throat, and her eyes grew round as all her fears returned.

The door opened, and a man stooped and entered the cabin. He straightened his body to his full height. Suddenly her heart was leaping and pounding.

"Stephen!"

"Who else? Did you think you'd been captured by pirates?" When she nodded, he said, "Did I not tell you I would save you from the monster Robert Morley?" He laughed jauntily as if he had made a joke.

"But I'm already his wife." She held up her hand, and the diamond ring sparkled. "You said you would save me from marriage to him."

"I admit my timing was not perfect. However, as a sailor's daughter you should know that the sea and winds are uncertain."

"My father will kill you for abducting me."

He laughed. "I think not. He'll have to catch me first."

"He will follow you."

"Life is more interesting when it becomes dangerous."

"You always joke."

"I joke because I'm happy that once more I have had the opportunity to rescue you, and that once more we are to share the same bed. Only this time it is a better bed and I intend us to make better use of it."

She sprang from the bed. "You did not rescue me this time. You kidnapped me."

"One and the same. You would have drowned had my man not saved you. I have saved you from death twice and now from this monster, Robert Morley, as well." Again he laughed, and she wondered if he bore her husband some grudge which she did not know about. "It seems, my dear, that you owe me a great deal," he added. His eyes were brilliant, as he moved toward her.

"If your man had not frightened me, I would never have fallen into that pool in the first place."

"Nevertheless, you did, and he saved you for me."

"You forget that I am now a married woman."

"The marriage has not yet been consummated."

"Oh, you are awful. How can you say such a thing?"

"Because it is the truth."

Easily he pulled her, in spite of her struggles, into his arms. He pushed her once more to the bed. Her mind was racing—desperate to stop him. He took her silence for acquiescence. His lips were in her hair.

Suddenly a suspicion that had been forming in her mind since he had entered the cabin jelled into a certainty.

"You came to the castle last night. I heard you talking to Father. And I saw you in the garden when you left. You could have saved me before the wedding took place but you didn't. I think my father agreed to pay you only after the wedding took place and that is why you waited to save me. He paid you *after* the wedding and then ... you ... you ... scoundrel that you are, abducted me. You're ... you're worse than a pirate!"

"Ah, you are referring to that conversation in the garden, the one you overheard when you thought I was bargaining with your father?"

"Yes."

"I would to God you'd never heard any of that! You misunderstood. I had no intention of helping your father marry you to another man. Katherine, I love you. I always have."

"I am no longer the gullible fool I was."

"I speak only the truth."

"Then if you're so willing to speak the truth, answer these questions. If you love me so much, what were you doing in Penzance with Sally Bodrugan? I saw you there as well as this ship. You were in Cornwall when you'd told Father you were in Devon. And what were you doing at the castle last night? Why didn't you come to me when I called you?" She moved across the room, opened the drawer of his desk, and pulled her miniature from it. "What are you doing with my miniature, the one my father supposedly sent Robert Morley?"

He studied her face closely before he answered. Her expression was set in anger, her eyes accusing.

"I see you kept yourself busy rummaging through my things," he said at last. He stalled. "I admired your miniature and your father had it copied for me before he sent it to your bridegroom." His voice was too smooth. She knew he was lying. "As for the rest, I've no intention of explaining myself to you. I've done nothing wrong."

"Nothing wrong? I think that in spite of all your jokes you are a very sinister person." She ignored the flash of light in his eyes that betrayed his rising anger. "I think you came to Cornwall for the express purpose of wrecking ships. You pretended to be appalled by wrecks, you pretended to be a fop who cared only for light courtships and poor jokes."

"Katherine, you go too far when you accuse me of wrecking ships, of murder." All warmth had left his voice. "I'm losing my patience with you."

"And that doesn't seem to be difficult for you. Once you used a knife on me in the garden."

"Remember it then!" He spanned the short distance between them, took her in his arms and shook her. She was afraid of him, as afraid as she had been in the garden. Then he caught himself, and folded his arms gently around her. His voice grew hoarse. "Katherine, I didn't want to quarrel with you tonight of all nights." His hands combed the silken fire of her hair. "God, I've missed you. I never knew I could miss a woman as I've missed you. And I've regretted that last night in the garden more than you can know. I'd been drinking with your father and when I saw you in Blake's arms—I was mad with jealousy, and I hurt you. I left because I couldn't face you. I've hoped and prayed you would forgive me." Gently he said, "Katherine, trust me—you must —there are things about myself, about my reasons for coming to Cornwall, I cannot share with you. My success in what I'm doing depends upon secrecy. But I'm no wrecker, please believe me."

In that moment, she did believe him. As always when he touched her, when he held her, she quivered with excitement. He stared deeply into her eyes, and she knew that he saw she was as eager as he was for this time they would have together. He led her once more to the bed, as if it were the most natural thing in the world.

There was a fierce banging at the door. "Captain, ye be needed on deck." Katherine recognized the voice of the man who had saved her from the marsh.

"Aye, Tummas," Stephen called angrily. "Ah, Katherine," he said gently, "saved again in the nick of time, are you not, my love?" He laughed softly. "But not for long. I'll only be a minute, I swear it!"

Chapter 13

When Stephen returned, he was serious. "It seems, love, my services will be needed on deck for quite some time. The weather is uncertain."

Lying against the soft pillows of his bed, Katherine stretched and curled her body languidly without knowing the torment she caused him. Her wrapper fell open, and the thin lawn of her chemise flowed over her provocative curves. She smiled up at him without realizing how such a sight affected him. She knew his power over her, but not yet her power over him.

"Must you leave me?" she purred.

"Yes, I have to take the wheel. No one knows these waters as I do. And because I have you on board, I plan to take every precaution." He was removing work clothes and oilskins from a locker as he talked. "Wreckers make use of nights such as this to practice their trade, as you know." He attempted to make his voice sound light. "I will not see you again until we sight Plymouth."

Then he was gone, carrying with him the tantalizing image of her body stretching gracefully in his bed. It was a vision that would haunt him all through the storm as he, lashed to the wheel so he would not be swept overboard by the waves crashing across the decks, steered the ship for Devon.

Katherine reached across the bed for another pillow and propped it on top of the others beneath her. Outside the world whitened and thunder boomed. The boat shook as it plowed through the crest of a high wave. The storm seemed to be rapidly worsening, but, snug in Stephen's bed, Katherine was not afraid. She felt safe with him at the wheel. He was a man who made his own destiny. No storm could stop him once he knew his way. He wanted her, and if his ship did not reach Plymouth safely, he would never have her. Plymouth—odd that his home should be the same as Robert Morley's. And Stephen always acted strangely whenever her husband's name was mentioned, as if he knew something he was keeping from her. What if Robert Morley learned the name of the man who had abducted her? She smiled. Perhaps Stephen would have to fight Robert Morley. But she would not worry about that now.

She could not have dreamed of a more perfect revenge against Robert Morley and her father than Stephen's abducting her. She pictured her father when he discovered her missing. He would be purple with rage . . . and Robert Morley . . . She did not know him, so she could not imagine his reaction. It served them right! Neither cared for her. All her father wanted was money, and Robert Morley had not cared enough to attend their wedding.

The ship lurched suddenly, falling heavily into the hollow of a wave, the high seas foaming across her decks. Katherine rose, and, realizing it would be impossible to keep her balance, she crawled across the pitching floor to the door. She opened it in time to see a waterfall showering through the partially opened hatch as Tummas lowered himself down the stairs.

"Mistress, ye must keep to y're cabin. Captain's orders."

"Are we going to sink?"

He laughed then, and she thought he was another such as Stephen—a man who thrived on danger.

"We be safe enough with the captain at the helm—even though he be not fully recovered."

Her questions cut off his words before he finished. "What? Is he ill? What's wrong with him?"

"Why, mistress, didn't ye know? He were very nearly murdered in Penzance. Cut down by rogues in the street and left in a stinking gutter for dead."

The wind howled and the ship slammed to a standstill as she hit a wall of water head-on. Then the vessel rolled. Katherine fell, and Tummas grabbed for her.

"Mistress, get back inside!" When she did not obey him, he growled, "Ain't it like a woman to be gabbing when our lives be hanging by a thread."

Three days and three nights passed before she saw Stephen again. When he did return, his eyes were shadowed from exhaustion, and he sagged against the door for support. Tummas undressed him and helped him to bed.

"The danger be past, mistress. I be the one to take the wheel now."

"You mean all this time he has had no sleep?"

"Aye." When he saw the concern in her eyes he added, "A sailor such as the captain can sleep in his boots with one eye closed and the other open to guide his ship."

"But he was wounded. How could you let him?"

"The captain be not as other men, mistress. There be no stopping him when his mind be set. Don't ye worry. He be as strong as a lion. Did he not live when I found him left for dead with the sword still in him? It were no more to him than a thorn in the paw of a lion."

When she returned to Stephen's bedside, he was as white as his nightshirt. She pictured him lying on the filthy cobbles of Penzance run through with a saber. It had been her fault, for she, by distrusting him, had driven him from the castle. If he had died, she would have been as guilty of his death as his murderer. She smoothed his hair from his brow. Oh, she would make it up to him. She loved him, no matter what he was, no matter what he had done. If she had to live with him without the sanctity of marriage, somehow she would find the strength to do so. She loved him and always would.

During the rest of the journey she tended to his every need. Tummas was right; Stephen was stronger than other men. But his strength made him a difficult patient.

"Do not grow accustomed to ordering me about, my pet," he said one morning after Tummas had just informed them that Plymouth had been sighted. "I'm so much improved, I'll soon turn the tables on you."

"And if you do, I'll soon have you back where I want you—in bed with a relapse. And I'll order you about just as I please." She laughed.

"For once we are of one mind," he said, reaching for her and pulling her into his arms. "For I too want you in bed."

188

"Stephen, why do you always deliberately misunderstand me and twist my words?"

"Because, my darling, you like to pretend you are as high-minded as a sister of the church, and it goads me when I know you want me as I want you."

"But I'm married to another man."

"And I've been married. Surely that's marriage enough to make our liaison correct."

"Stephen, you are scandalous. And you delight in being so. What if my husband finds you and kills you?"

He pushed her from him and laughed as if she had made a fine joke. At last he said, "Somehow, my darling, I have no fear of that happening."

And as always when the subject turned to her husband, she thought Stephen knew something she did not.

Their first night in Plymouth they intended to remain on board ship. As Stephen was fully recovered from his exhaustion, Katherine thought she would not be able to put him off much longer. Tonight he would come to her, insistent and demanding, and there would be no stopping him.

During supper Stephen seemed impatient for the meal to be over, and she sensed he was eager to be alone with her. She found herself seeking ways to prolong the meal. His black eyes, intense and assessing, missing nothing, were too often on her. She felt shy and nervous. Conversation was impossible. Every time he looked across the table at her, her skin burned as if she had a fever. She could not meet his gaze without flushing, and she spent the meal toying with her goblet of ale—staring into it, holding it and rotating her wrist so that the liquid swished like a miniature whirlpool.

At last a large, brown hand wrapped around the tiny white one and stilled her motion. Firmly he drew her hand away from the goblet.

Her eyes met his, and she grew warm. Her pulse quickened. She was trembling, and he gripped her fingers more tightly. The moment was charged with tension. All the excitement of the unknown, of the yet to be discovered, lay before them. Katherine was afraid he would find her wanting, and Stephen was boldly confident.

"Katherine, darling, you have nothing to fear." He leaned forward and kissed her forehead to reassure her.

He pushed his chair back, and she knew that even though the main course had not yet been served, supper was over. Then Tummas, letters in hand, came barging through the door and broke the spell.

"There be news from your family, Captain—from Lady Constance."

Did a knowing look pass between the two men? Taking the letters, Stephen sat back scowling with impatience. He tore open the seal of one of them and read. He paused and looked up as if the news were too incredible to believe and then forced himself to reread it once more. Once more he looked up, and she could see he was visibly shaken.

In answer to the question in her eyes, he said, "It's my father. He's ill, although there seems to be no imminent danger. Still, it comes as a shock to no sooner arrive in port and . . ." He hesitated for a moment.

He opened a second letter and read it. The contents of this letter seemed to please him, for he smiled. "You will forgive me if I leave you? There is someone I must see tonight . . . before I see my family." He seemed eager to be gone at once.

She did not see him again until the next morning. She knew he had left the ship, and that he had not returned until the sun came up.

In spite of his sleepless night and the news about his father, he seemed refreshed and in the best of moods when he came to her the next morning. She could not stop the unpleasant doubts that nagged her. Where had he gone? Had he spent the night with Lady Constance?

When he joined her for breakfast, he proposed they journey to an inn called The Three Feathers, where he always kept rooms hired.

"Isn't that rather extravagant—to keep rooms even when you are not using them?" she asked.

"When you know me better you will find that I am a man of extravagant tastes. In the past when I spent time in Plymouth, I was not always received by my family." Her eyebrows arched with curiosity. "There was a difference of opinion, a family matter my father and I disagreed about. I shall explain it to you sometime."

"The disagreement has been mended?"

"Yes."

"And still you keep the rooms?"

"They are more convenient to the harbor and, therefore, to my business."

"And more convenient to keep a mistress who

cannot be received by one's family. Am I to become such a mistress, always kept in the background, some-one . . ." Her voice caught.

"Ah, I see where this is leading." He met her troubled gaze. "No, my darling, no." They were in one another's arms. "I promise you. But there is some-thing I must explain to you before I can take you to my family, something that is going to require a great deal of understanding on your part. As you know, I've just learned my father is ill. As soon as I secure rooms for you, I must go to him, and prepare him to accept you, just as I must prepare you to accept him."

Katherine thought again of Lady Constance, and wondered about her relationship to Stephen. She pushed her unpleasant thoughts from her mind and rested her head against his shoulder. If only she could stop doubting him.

Later, in spite of her doubts, Katherine enjoyed the ride to the inn. She gazed at the soft, lush Devon countryside and did not miss her stark Cornish home-land.

Plymouth hummed with activity, and Katherine, staring in wonder at the new sights, did not notice that Stephen's mood had darkened. Sights that were novel and thrilling to her were familiar and dull to him—and filled with painful memories.

As they rode into the courtyard of the inn, their host ran to greet them and held their horses' reins so they could easily dismount. He was a small, fat man who, at the sight of Stephen, became very agitated. His words tumbled out of his mouth—an incoherent jumble of unctuous compliments. His hands were trembling and Stephen's mount shied.

"Stop your shaking, host, and hold the horse steady," Stephen demanded impatiently. "You're making him skittish."

As he swung himself to the ground, Katherine saw him wince. Perhaps his painful wound was making him so impatient.

"Your rooms, my lord, oh . . ." The landlord's flabby jowl quivered and he raised his hands heavenward as if to solicit help.

The man's sudden movement jerked the bit in Stephen's horse's mouth, and the animal neighed wildly and pawed the ground. Furious, Stephen grabbed the reins from the man and patted the horse's white-starred nose, speaking softly to soothe him. When the horse quieted, he turned on the landlord.

"Fool, have you no sense at all about animals? And what is this about my rooms?"

"My lord, if I had known. It be so long—twelvemonth since you were here. I let them to a party of travelers only last night."

"You let my rooms? We have a standing agreement, you and I. And it seems to me you've done this to me before. You take my money and rent my rooms to others! You must order this party of travelers to vacate my rooms at once—before I throw them out myself!"

"Your lordship, I have other rooms."

"But none so fine as the Queen's Room."

"None worthy of your lordship or his lady. That be God's truth."

Stephen drew his sword from his scabbard and brandished it menacingly. He laughed harshly, as if he enjoyed frightening the landlord, and Katherine saw that the landlord was truly terrified. His eyes bobbed rapidly in their fat pockets as they watched the swirling flourish of blade. With the point of his sword Stephen pricked the doublet in the middle of the man's round belly. The man gasped in terror and gave a little yelp, trying unsuccessfully to suck in his protruding stomach.

"You make an easy target, host," Stephen laughed. To Katherine his voice and laughter seemed satanic. Here was a side of him she had seen only once before— in the garden.

He sheathed his sword and the man sighed heavily. "The lady and I will wait in the parlor while you prepare my rooms," Stephen said. "Remember, I do not like to be kept waiting."

"Yes . . . yes . . . my lord."

The man rushed inside and Stephen reached up to Katherine to help her dismount.

"I think you were a little hard on him, Stephen," she chided, careful to keep her voice gentle. "For a moment I thought you actually enjoyed bullying him."

"And so I did, love." The light in his eyes was fierce. "You must learn that I let neither man nor woman take advantage of me."

The landlord ushered them into the Queen's Room, so named because Mary Tudor was reputed to have once slept there. A fire leapt in the grate, lighting the room with a flickering glow. A warming pan had been placed beneath the sheets of the bed.

"I have a suckling pig on the spit and mutton—your favorite pies, my lord."

"Everything seems to be in order now, host," Stephen agreed. "Leave us." He turned to Katherine. "I must go now, love. You may take your meals in a private dining room. Tummas will be glad to show you Plymouth. He will see to your every need."

He seemed eager to be gone and she wondered again about Lady Constance.

"When will you return?"

"When I can. My father is very ill. I fear he can't last long at his age."

"Last night you said there was no imminent danger."

"That was before I . . ."

She moved away from him to the window, not wanting him to know how much she wanted to go with him.

"Katherine, is something wrong?"

Her voice shook with tears. "No."

"But there is!" He was beside her at once, his hand gently turning her face so that her tear-filled eyes met him. "You're crying."

"Because I feel so cheap to be here with you like this when I'm married to another man. Your father is ill and you have to leave me here as if you were ashamed of me." Although she didn't say it aloud, she also wept because of the other women she imagined he kept rooms for—especially Lady Constance.

"Katherine, darling, that's not why I'm leaving you." He held her tightly, murmuring endearments. "My dearest wife—" The words thundered in her brain.

"Wife?"

He hesitated, and then said easily, "Yes, you are my wife as truly as if I stood beside you at the altar and took the vows when you did. You are the woman I want beside me for the rest of my life—my woman until death parts us."

"Still, I am married to Robert Morley, a man I loathe."

He paused, considering his answer carefully. Sunshine fell full upon her face, and he saw her jaw tighten as her father's did when he was determined. Her eyes had narrowed with dislike as she spoke the name *Morley*.

"Forget Robert Morley! What matters is that you love me, and I love you. We will live together as man and wife, and someday soon, I promise you, my family will receive you as my lawful wife."

"Do you intend to kill my husband?"

He laughed. "You are impossible! Did I not just tell you, I *am* your husband?"

"What you said is romantic nonsense. You have been so long at Court that you think you have only to say pretty words to a woman, and she will fall into your arms. You must surely be a master at seducing women. But I am not as foolish as the rest."

"No, you are not at all foolish. You are the only woman for me." He kissed her lips lightly, then more passionately. "I would to God I did not have to leave you now," he whispered hoarsely.

Then he was gone. She stood motionless at the window listening to his retreating footsteps on the stairs, and watching as he painfully mounted his horse and rode away. When he was out of sight, she was desolate.

Would this be her life now—watching him ride

away and waiting endlessly for his return? Oh, what was to become of her? She wanted him—yes! But she wanted *marriage* to him. Her upbringing had not prepared her for this sort of life. For a long time she stared down upon the empty courtyard. The wind gusting up dried her cheeks.

The next day Tummas came with a note from Stephen. She tried to decipher the scrawling letters: Dearest—Father grave, do not know how long . . . The rest was scribble. She wadded the note, threw it into the fire, and watched it blacken and crumple into a ball of flame. So he was not coming. She twisted the diamond ring on her finger and sighed.

Perhaps she only imagined that the other guests at the inn avoided her deliberately. When she entered the parlor, they hastily made excuses and left. If they came upon her suddenly in the courtyard, their expressions froze, their voices dying in mid-sentence.

One afternoon, at considerable risk to her own person, she rescued a small boy from the flying hooves of a horse. She received a scowl for thanks from the boy's mother, who quickly snatched the child from her.

"Tummas," she asked the next morning, "do you think the guests are angry because Stephen insisted I have the Queen's Room?"

"Nay, they be more afraid of ye than angry, mistress, because ye be a friend to the captain."

"Afraid of me, of the captain?" He nodded. "But why?"

"That be for him to say, mistress."

* * *

One week later Stephen returned shortly after midnight. Katherine, who had long been in bed, awakened as his key turned in the lock. He entered the room holding a candle high in one hand, and she saw his face clearly outlined in its circular glow.

Light and shadow transformed his familiar features. His black eyes were liquid crystal—cold and bright; his mouth curved into a humorless smile. Setting the candle on the mantel he threw his gloves on the high-backed chair beside him and fumbled impatiently with his cloak. She sensed that his mood was dark and wondered uneasily if she were the cause of it.

"Stephen? What are you doing? What's wrong?"

At the sound of her voice, his smile twisted, and he was almost himself again. He tossed his soaking cloak onto the chair and moved toward the bed.

"What do you think I'm doing? The pirate has come to claim his prize." The flame of the candle was lambent in his eyes, but his voice was cold. "And as for what's wrong—you've my family to thank for putting me into this infernal mood."

Her fingertips were on his lips. "Is your father . . ."

"No!" His voice was sharp like a knife slicing the air.

"Then . . . what . . . what happened?"

"It's not what they did this time. It's what they've done in the past and what they'd do again. The only time I ever needed them to stand beside me, they prejudged me and turned me out." His eyes raked over her and became accusing. "And you, my dear, are another such as they."

"What have I done?"

"Oh, you'd turn against me fast enough. Look how you prejudged your husband. You don't even know him and yet you believe him guilty of murder."

"But you know as well as I that he is a murderer."

"You see what I mean."

"But everyone knows—"

"Everyone can go to the devil!" His hands gripped her arms; his voice was passionate with anger.

"Stephen, what is wrong? You're hurt."

He released her and moved away. "Oh, I was a fool to let my family talk me into going to Cornwall in the first place. Then I should never have met you, never have let myself in for—"

"Stephen, what are you talking about? You're not making any sense."

He turned on her. His tone was flippant, but his eyes blazed. "A thousand pardons, love, for bothering you with all this. But remember one thing: it hurts like hell when the people you care for turn against you."

He pulled his shirt over his head and threw it to the floor. He was moving toward her.

"Stephen, what are you—"

"Can't you guess? Did you think I rode through this storm to satisfy myself with talk? Tonight I intend to have what is mine. I found you in a storm, do you remember?" His eyes upon her were magnetic. "And it was storming the night of that wreck, the night I knew I must have you, the night you hung from that cliff. And tonight when it began to thunder I left my family and returned to you."

He pulled her to him and his lips were savage.

"No, Stephen. No! Not like this." He ignored her

pleas and kissed her again brutally. She was deeply offended by his manner, by his failure to care for her feelings.

"That night in Penzance when I lay dying in the street, it was you that kept me alive. I vowed that I would live so that you would be mine."

His lips on hers were hot, demanding. She began to struggle, but he held her more tightly with arms as hard and strong as granite. She did not want him to make love to her in his present mood, driven as he was by anger rather than love. She twisted and slid, but he paid no attention and pulled her under him. One of his hands reached for the neckline of her chemise and tore it, shredding the thin silk so that she lay beneath him naked in the candlelight, her body gleaming like polished ivory as she shrank against the bed. His eyes went over her slowly. He pressed his coarse cheek in the hollow between her breasts.

She cried out, and his lips were instantly on hers, muffling her cries. She felt the thick hairs of his chest, the dampness of his skin still wet from the rain, the incredible heat of his body as it covered hers.

His kisses became urgent, possessive, and ruthless, and suddenly her resistance was melting. She fought him, but her resolve weakened. She wanted him; she had always wanted him and he knew it. She opened her mouth and returned his kisses. Her response excited him more.

She thought, He only wants me physically because he is angry, not because he loves me. He's probably felt this for many women. But I love him and I want him. That will have to be enough.

She thought no more as he drew her with him into a dark world of fierce passion, where the feel of his skillful hands was delight, where his very breath burned her flesh.

A draft from the raging gusts outside seeped through the window. The candle flickered and went out, but they did not notice. They were lost in a timeless space that was joy, fear, and madness. Their lips were bruising and tender, their embraces fierce and gentle. Some force more powerful than they—as ancient as the human race—directed them onward, deeper and deeper until they became one.

Their passion calmed, Katherine began to weep, and Stephen—all his anger gone—folded her gently into his arms and kissed her tenderly.

"This time," he said softly, "it will be for you." He kissed her again, slowly, deeply. His lips followed the soft lines of her flesh, every curve, every hollow. Her breath quickened, and her skin glowed with warmth. Never, in all her life, had she felt so complete and happy.

She fell asleep in his arms only to be awakened by his lips again. Oh, how she loved him—physically, mentally, in every way a woman can love a man. She had never imagined love could be like this. If only he were her husband—but she would not think of that now when she was so happy. Once more she slept.

Much later Katherine stirred restlessly, awakening again to the sound of loud voices at the door. She reached across the bed to touch Stephen but there was only a warm indentation in the feather mattress where he had lain.

The room was bright with sunlight, the air crisply cool and fresh with the scent of rain. Already sounds drifted up from the courtyard.

To Katherine it was the most beautiful morning of her life. She yawned and stretched languidly, wishing Stephen would come back to bed. She remembered his kisses, his hands upon her, the feel of his body, and she smiled contentedly.

The voices at the door grew louder. She recognized the landlord's voice—high-pitched and quavering.

"But my Lord Morley . . . Lord Morley . . . You don't understand! It were not my wish to wake you so early. It be your father—he be dying. You were to return at once to your home."

Fear gripped her heart before understanding dawned. Her husband Robert Morley had somehow discovered she was here with Stephen, and had come to find them. He meant to kill Stephen and would probably kill her as well! Sitting up, she strained to hear, and suddenly realization burst upon her. Stephen spoke roughly, but it was not Stephen. It was Robert Morley. Stephen *was* Robert Morley, her husband!

"Damnation, man! Must you shout as if I've no ears? And didn't I tell you not to call me that with her so near?" The landlord answered in nervous gibberish. Lord Morley continued, "Saddle our horses, host, and prepare our breakfast at once."

Katherine did not realize that her eyes were large with fear, that her mouth hung open with horror. The door clicked shut, and Stephen approached the bed, moving toward her with the easy grace of a large cat. When he saw her expression, he stopped short.

"And so, now you know." He watched her face closely, as if her next words were immensely important to him.

She now saw Stephen in a new light. He was as ruggedly handsome as ever, standing perfectly still, his great body tense with expectation. His jet-black hair was tousled from sleep, and his unwavering gaze never left her face. Suddenly she saw that his eyes were watchful, hopeful. He seemed to hang on her next words, hoping she would say . . . What did a man like him hope for? He was a monster!

Her brain whirled with torment. He was Robert Morley! He and her father had obviously conspired to trick her with an elaborate masquerade, the story of a distant kinsman—ha—when all the time . . . If it weren't so awful, it would be funny. Her father must be smug with satisfaction; everything had worked out exactly as he had wanted. Once more she had played the part of a gullible fool. Strangely enough, what most enraged her was the thought of her father's gloating triumph. Her eyebrows drew together in a cold frown.

When she said nothing, Stephen smiled a slow, deliberate smile, reminding her of his nephew, Jason Morley.

"It's a shock, I know, but perhaps it's better this way, to have everything out in the open, to have an end to pretense," he said.

When he moved toward her, she cried out, "Don't come near me! Don't ever touch me again!"

He stopped, his jaw hardening.

"Do you know," he began quietly, "you look exactly as my mother looked the night she accused me of killing my first wife, Monica. My own mother!" He hesitated, and when she did not answer him he said, "All these months I wanted to explain the way things were to you. I did not want the past to come between us. But you were so set against me."

He continued to speak, but she no longer listened. If only he would leave her, perhaps she could sort things out. Her emotions were a jumble of anger, resentment, and shock. She felt stupid for having been so easily duped. But Robert was Stephen, and Stephen Robert, and she had thought herself in love with him. She had just spent the night in his arms!

He had been a skillful lover, and was obviously an equally skillful liar. How much of their relationship was pretense, how much reality? Was he, like her father, motivated only by greed, marrying her solely for money? She recalled how frequently he had been with Sally Bodrugan, how he had gone to Lady Constance. He had left her alone for a week, ostensibly to visit his sick father, but had he been with other women instead? And what of last night? Had his ardor been love or lust?

"You haven't heard a word I've said," Stephen—now Robert—finished wearily. "Like all the rest, you are ready to condemn me." Still she said nothing. "Aren't you, Katherine? Aren't you?" His eyes were fixed on her lips, awaiting her answer.

As he moved toward her, she blurted out, "I . . . I . . . don't know. You've tricked me, lied to me, and I just don't know any longer what I believe. How can you ask for my trust now?"

"Because, Wife, I need it. I must have it!"

His eyes were fierce, and she remembered the night in the garden when he had cut her gown with his knife. His eyes had been fierce then too. She remembered how he had bullied the landlord with his sword and enjoyed doing it. She remembered Tummas' rough treatment of her—under orders from him. Her eyes traced the slashes on his chest. If he were the innocent he claimed, why had someone tried to murder him?

Robert advanced upon her, and she cowered with terror. He seized her, and the blankets fell away, revealing her nakedness. His eyes drifted lazily to her breasts, and she trembled in fear that he would hurt her, that he would use her again as he had last night.

"And so you are afraid of me?" His voice was soft, his words oddly measured. His face suddenly blackened with fury, and she trembled more violently, maddening him all the more. For one long moment he glared at her, then he threw her back onto the bed.

"You must get dressed, Lady Morley. We've a long ride to Morley Court. You'll like my family, for you and they have much in common." He rummaged through her clothes. "Here. Get up." When she did not obey, he dragged her naked from the bed. "Put this on."

She pulled the chemise over her head. His hands were on her, wrapping her corset around her waist, pulling the cords so viciously that she cried out. "You see, I know well enough how to dress a woman. I've had enough practice—with women who did not shrink from my touch." She shook with fear. "I see my second wife will be like my first—afraid of me." He laughed softly.

"Yes . . . yes . . . I'm afraid of you. And for good reason. You delight in bullying, terrifying, and . . . and . . . murdering."

He twisted her roughly in his arms, and his hands enclosed her throat. His eyes were savage with hatred. "You said that to me once before. Don't ever, ever say it again."

He released her and she fell backward. He stalked across the room and slammed the door, his boots echoing heavily on the stairs as he ran down them two at a time. His orders reverberated in the courtyard.

At last the roar subsided and she heard the twittering notes of a lark in the nearby branch of a tree as it sang of the glorious morning. The fragile, beautiful music shattered her control and she collapsed onto the bed in tears.

Breakfast was a silent ordeal, as was the long ride to Morley Court. Lush hills painted with colorful sprays of coltsfoot and crimson-tipped daisies rolled down to a misty sea. At a shallow stream butterbur and purple catkins bloomed on the banks. But Katherine was aware of nothing save the grim-faced man who rode beside her and the leaden ache in her heart.

How had everything gone wrong so quickly? Only last night—she must never think of last night again! But she could not stop herself. Last night he had been gentle, tender and she had thought he loved her. No, she would be a fool to believe that. He was a skilled lover, a skilled actor. He knew what a woman wanted in bed. He had only pretended tenderness.

As they emerged from the trees into the open, he

grabbed the reins of her horse. Without speaking he helped her dismount and led her to the top of the hill. In the distance a high cliff was crowned with the stark, gray, machicolated towers of his home.

"Welcome to Morley Court, Wife," he said softly.

She turned sharply to face him, her mind furious with revolt. He towered over her, ready to dominate her, as his castle dominated its landscape. She bit back her words.

Chapter 14

The rest of the day was nightmare. Morley Court—darkened and silent—was already a house of mourning as its occupants awaited the death of the old man upstairs. A servant led Katherine and Robert up the staircase—broad, steep, and stately with an elaborately carved wooden balustrade—and ushered them into the sickroom.

Robert rushed at once to a woman huddling by the bed who half rose to meet him. She was tall, almost as tall as her son, and elegant in a gown of black silk shot with silver threads. The woman's tear-filled black eyes—Robert's own eyes grown older and sadder—observed Katherine for a long moment in silent assessment. She seemed to see much in a glance, and Katherine was reminded of Robert, who sometimes seemed able to read her heart and soul. The woman extended her hand to Katherine.

"Welcome home, child. I'm sorry you had to come at such . . ." She looked away, disconcerted because she had lost the thread of her speech. Looking lost and forlorn, she released Katherine's hand and sank once more into the chair beside her husband's bed.

Robert's father, a shrunken form in the great bed,

feebly smiled his satisfaction when he learned who Katherine was. His breathing was torturous, and Robert's mother wept continuously, as if she suffered as much as he. Theirs had obviously been a happy marriage. Even though Katherine barely knew them, their unhappiness deeply depressed her. When she thought she could stand it no longer, Robert led her from the room. She almost thought his gesture thoughtful, but she knew Robert Morley was incapable of thoughtfulness.

Katherine rested in the beautiful bedroom she had been given. Morley Court was a much grander, though older, home than Cranston Castle. Doubtless her father had been impressed with it. Her eyes flitted across the room to the ceiling patterned in deep relief; the expanse of wide, latticed windows; the brilliant tapestries, paintings, and furniture; and the thick oriental carpet covering the floor. Her father had seen this ostentatious display of wealth, and his greed had made him want it for his own. Now his grandchildren would be Morleys; his blood would be part of this magnificence.

And she would bear children to a man she despised. She shuddered and was drawing the coverlets closer, when a knock sounded faintly at the door. Katherine jumped, but before she could answer an old woman dragging one lame foot, her face like wrinkled paper, hobbled into the room and bobbed an awkward curtsey. Seeing Katherine, she smiled a curiously bright and youthful smile. Katherine warmed to her instantly.

"I be wanting to see the young lord's new bride," the woman said. She tucked a faded wisp of hair beneath her cap. "Ye do be a beauty." When Katherine said nothing, the old woman continued, "I be Winnie, the young lord's nanny when he were a lad. He were such a good child. Never give me a mite of trouble."

The old woman stared at her expectantly, as if she was eager to gossip. Suddenly Katherine was as curious as the old servant.

"Have you been with the family always?"

"Since I were a girl. I don't have to tell ye, there were much rejoicing in spite of the old lord's poor health, when Sir Robin—Robin be his pet name—come home last week and told the family of his marriage. All but William were happy."

"William? Who's he?"

"William be the second son, and the old lord did say he were going to leave his shipping business and his holdings in Kent to William if Sir Robin refused to marry ye."

"Oh."

"Not that he didn't want to marry ye, but now it be settled as it should be. William's to have the business in London and a ship or two of his own and Robin the rest."

"So he married me for money?"

The old woman raised a quivering hand to her ear. "Eh?"

"Nothing." Still the woman couldn't hear. "NOTH-ING!" Katherine shouted, not knowing that her stubborn chin looked just like her father's. The lust for money seemed to control her life, she thought. Robert's marriage to her had meant no more to him than another lucrative business proposition. And now that he had married her, what did he think? Had he decided that marriage to her was too high a price to pay for his inheritance? She thought of the night she had spent in his arms, a night of rapture for her but what had it been for him?

The old woman scrutinized the young woman's face, and drew her own conclusions for the unhappiness she saw.

"It be not wise to go against the young lord, Lady Morley," she said gently. "That were what his first wife done, and ye know her story. He were always one to be worse if ye look for the badness in him, Robin were." She hesitated, as if to draw her thoughts together. "A wise wife be trusting in her husband and in his courage. Ye be kind to the young lord. Don't ye thwart him, but obey him, cherish him. And when he knows ye love him, ye'll command his love as well. He were a soft-hearted boy, mistress, and he be no different now. Only his life since he were a boy were hard on him. Well, good luck to ye."

The bony hands patted her kindly in farewell, and when Katherine looked up the old woman had gone. She did not consider the old woman's advice about being kind to Robert, thinking only of the wealth that would now be his because of their marriage. The old woman's words echoed in her brain, "It be not wise to go against the young lord. That were what his first wife done. And ye know her story."

Was Robert really evil? Did she really know him at all? Where was the man she had first thought him to be, the man who had nursed her for two days in the Bodrugan cottage, the man who had refrained from seducing her because he wanted to protect her from himself. That afternoon he would eventually marry her, yet he had not taken her; he had waited until marriage. Why? She had thought him a man who loved life, a man with a sense of humor. Who was he really?

The world placed the blame for Monica Morley's death on her husband, yet he insisted he was innocent. Was he? Katherine knew him to be a man of complex character. He was fearless, passionate, he loved jokes and had a violent temper. If he were angry enough was he capable of murder?

She had to get away to think. Too much had happened too quickly. She no longer knew what she felt or thought. Only yesterday she had been deeply in love. Could such a powerful feeling change in so short a time? Still, if those feelings had been based on a clever pretense, if the man she had thought she loved did not exist . . .

Oh, she could make no sense of it, no sense at all. She dashed from her room, and just as she reached the landing, Robert came out of his father's room and closed the door. His face was ashen with grief. Seeing his sorrow, she forgot for the moment her fear of him.

"Your father? He's . . ."

"Yes. It's over." He paused, and then went on. "We had our differences but now that he's gone only the good times seem important. Funny—I think he felt the same about me in the end. I didn't always measure up to his infernal standards, I didn't always do what he wanted, but I think in the end . . ." His voice trailed off. "His last words were about us, about our future."

"What did he say?"

"He said you were very beautiful, as beautiful as

Mother was when he brought her home to Morley Court." His voice broke with anguish. "He said that I was lucky to have you for my wife, and that he wanted us to be happy."

"Oh. I'm sorry he's dead." Her voice was flat and emotionless. "I know it's a loss." She felt awkward, and could think of nothing more to say. She only wanted to get away from him and be alone. Feeling sympathy for him in addition to what she already felt made her even more confused.

He moved toward her, as if to take her in his arms for comfort. But she was determined to avoid his touch. How could she possibly think when he held her?

"No . . . Robert . . . I—not now." In a sudden rush she backed toward the stairs, her palms sliding along the slick wood of the railing, her slipper feeling cautiously for the first stair. She simply had to get away. If he held her—even for a moment—she would be lost.

When she moved backward, he thought she was afraid of him. His face twisted into an expression she would carry with her always. He was stricken with a grief more profound than the sorrow he felt for his father's death. His was the face of a man utterly bereft, a man who had lost everything, a man who no longer knew where to turn.

She had rejected him when he needed her most, and by doing so she had hurt him terribly. Before she could do or say anything to make amends, he stiffened proudly with anger. He looked at her through eyes luminous with pain and yearning—as if he'd lost everything by losing her, and her heart softened as she realized how deeply he loved her. Surely a man who looked at her like that had not married her for money. Whatever he had done, he loved her—and she loved him.

Her eyes grew moist with tenderness; her smile became gentle. She would take him in her arms and comfort him. She would beg his forgiveness for having been so childishly set against him. She'd been a fool to judge him without listening to his explanation. She'd been wrong—oh, so wrong—about so many things. The agonized expression on his face had changed everything.

But he did not notice the change in her. The long day at his father's beside, waiting for the old man to die, had been a strain. His grief, combining with the sharp disappointment of her cool rejection, was more than he could stand. His features hardened, his eyes ablaze with rage. "Damn you!" he said at last. "Damn you! But I don't know why I'm blaming you. I always knew what you'd do once you found out. I was a fool to fall into the same trap twice. Your coming into my life provides the supreme irony of my life. Well, never mind—I love you, and you're so indifferent to me, you won't even listen when I say I'm innocent. Now when I need you, you turn against me."

He advanced upon her, and she saw that he was angrier than she had ever seen him. But this time she was not afraid. She understood the source of his anger. She had hurt him, inflicting pain on top of pain, and it was more than he could bear.

"Robert . . . I'm . . ." She loosened her grip on the bannister and reached for him, wanting to

215

apologize, yearning to soothe his pain and anger. But as she leaned forward, the toe of her slipper caught on the edge of the stair and she lost her footing, falling backward. She grabbed wildly for the bannister, for anything that would break her fall. Robert was a blur of motion as he rushed to save her. He was agile and fast. She was in his arms, and he was steadying her. His heart pounded close to her ear. Looking beyond his shoulder, down the steep stairs, she saw that they were the stairs of her dream—descending forever into the gloom of the unlit hall.

"If I pushed you, Wife, or let you go, you would fall."

He laughed as she clung to him, but she felt safe.

"You could have let me fall of my own accord," she murmured.

Robert carefully replaced her hands on the railing, not releasing her until he was absolutely sure she had her balance.

"True. Still, it would never do for me to lose my second wife in the same way I lost my first." Deliberately, he made his voice casual. But she had seen the panic in his eyes when he thought she would fall. He had reached for her and crushed her to him as if she were very dear to him.

"Is this the staircase where . . ."

"Yes."

Involuntarily she shivered. Her nightmare had nearly come true. But he misinterpreted her trembling and his fury returned.

"I see you are afraid of me, Wife. You believe everything you've heard. Continue to do so. Your feelings will make no difference to me. Remember this: you are my wife, my property, to use in any way I please. Everything that is yours is now mine, and I will expect obedience from you in everything. Everything—do you understand me?" When she said nothing, he continued, "And I intend to enjoy my rights as a husband in your bed whether you like it or not."

"You would force me—"

"Of course. But not tonight with my father lying dead in his bed. We'll stay here until the funeral and then return to Cornwall. I have not yet finished my business there."

He descended the stairs ahead of her and dashed from the house. She heard him outside calling for his horse.

Had she lost him because she'd turned from him in his hour of need? His horse pounded the earth in a mad gallop as he rode away, echoing the pounding of her hopeless heart.

She ran down the stairs, and into the courtyard after him, calling his name. But he never looked back. He vanished into the twilight haze, and she was alone in a bleak world.

The morning after Lord Morley's funeral, Robert and Katherine left for Cornwall. Neither took any joy in the beautiful morning. The sun gilded the horizon, the air was warm and wet, and the hedgerows were netted with glistening cobwebs.

Katherine stared blindly ahead, and Robert spoke to her only when necessary. Since their quarrel on the landing, he seemed to have completely lost interest in her and avoided her whenever possible.

As the days passed and his disinterest persisted, all her doubts about him returned. She wondered again if he had ever loved her. If he had loved her once, perhaps her rejection of him after his father's death had turned that love sour. Perhaps the only reason he stayed with her was to satisfy his family and protect his inheritance.

When they stopped at inns along the way, he secured separate rooms for them. She retired early and waited expectantly for him, but he never came. He always remained below drinking with the other guests. One night quite late she heard him mount the stairs and pause before her door, but he did not enter. In the mornings his eyes were red from exhaustion and drink. She wondered if he drank to forget her or to endure her.

She longed to apologize to him, to beg his forgiveness for her behavior. But every time she approached him, his cold gaze made her break off stammering. An invisible chasm seemed to divide them, and with the passing of each day it widened.

At last they reached Cranston Castle, wrapped in fog, and Sir Cranston received them in his closet.

"Welcome home, Daughter, Robin my son." Her father beamed with joy. At the sight of her gloomy expression, he said, "A wise woman begins her marriage with a better attitude than yours, Daughter." To Robert he added, "'Tis my fault, Robin. I've spoiled her." When Robert made no answer, Sir Cranston eyed the pair for a long, intense moment before changing the subject. "There were three wrecks from that storm that blew up the night you left. The guard posted at The Queen's Light was overpowered and bludgeoned—left for dead. The cowardly fool has recovered but he won't tell us who did it to him. He's afraid he'll be murdered in his bed if he talks."

"Damn! I was gone when you needed me!"

"There's no help for it now. I've had the servants prepare a suite of rooms for you in the west wing. They command an excellent view of the sea and of The Queen's Light."

Stephen's eyes raked coldly over his wife. "I think, sir, you should give Katherine her old room. I'll take my room at the cottage."

"You are married now."

"Still, I would prefer the arrangement I suggested." The two men stared knowingly at one another.

There was a long, awkward moment of silence.

"As you wish," Sir Cranston said at last. "Will you excuse me for a minute. I've remembered something I need to do. I'll find Sally so she can prepare your rooms at the cottage."

Sir Cranston swiftly crossed the room, leaving Katherine to wonder if Sally were the reason her husband preferred the humble cottage to rooms with her. Once he had said he liked his women warm and willing. Was Sally such a woman? If she had possessed a fortune, would he have married her instead?

Robert sprawled comfortably upon a sofa near the fire to await his father-in-law's return, and Katherine stood near the windows, looking out to sea. Once, when she turned suddenly, she saw him watching her with an alert, eager, waiting look on his face. His face changed swiftly into an unreadable blank.

Could it mean that he cared for her? Before thinking, she began eagerly, "I could stay with you at the cottage."

His expression did not change, and his voice was unenthusiastic as usual. "Katherine, you never cease to surprise me. I can see you've weighed the merit of your father's advice about improving your attitude toward our marriage and decided to follow it for a change. But I've no need of your charity. I'll do quite well alone."

"Robert . . . I . . . I . . ."

"I see no need to discuss this further. You're being most generous, but I've no need for it."

She turned from him quickly before he could see her tears. He saw only that the line of her back stiffened, that the hand she raised quivered as she fumbled with the folds of the drapes.

The watchful, puzzling glint came back into his eyes, but he said nothing.

Husband and wife passed a quarter of an hour in uncomfortable silence as they waited for Sir Cranston's return. When he did return, the two men became absorbed in conversation, talking of ships and wrecking. They seemed relieved when Katherine excused herself and returned to her room. She undressed and slipped into her bed.

She was home—back in her old room. It was unchanged, and yet because she was changed everything was changed. She stretched, tossed, and rolled, yet sleep would not come. She was a married woman, and she was wretched because Robert had lost interest in her. She wanted him; she needed his forgiveness.

She was still awake when a key rattled in the lock

of her door. She sat up, hearing the heavy, familiar tread of her husband's boots on the carpet. He parted the bed curtains. He was already bare-chested.

"I thought you were going to stay in the cottage."

"Did I not tell you I intend to enjoy my rights as a husband in your bed whether you like it or not?"

"But you've been so cold, so distant. You act as if you don't care anything for me, as though you don't love—"

"What has love to do with making love?" His voice was brusque. He gathered her in his arms. "You are my wife. You belong to me."

His lips were on hers, and she kissed him fiercely, her need as great as his. The warmth of her response inflamed him.

"Oh, Katherine . . ."

Their passion became a possessive force that drove and shook them. For a timeless moment everything that had divided them melted away. For Katherine it was a shattering experience. She lost herself to him. It was like fainting, like dying. She became a part of him. But what was it like for him? He gave her no clue.

At last they lay in silence without touching, and becoming herself once more she reddened with shame. Did he think her passion coarse? Did he despise her? What was he thinking?

After they had lain for a time in silence, Robert arose and fumbled in the darkness for his clothes. She reached for him to draw him back to bed, and as always the touch of him excited her.

He paused for a long moment, then shrugged her hand from his arm.

"I see, Wife, you are like me," he said. "You can make love when you do not love, and still enjoy it. At least, we are compatible in bed."

Before she could reply, he carelessly slung his doublet and cloak over his shoulder. He was going—going without knowing how she loved him. She heard him whistling as he descended the stair. Was he happy that he was leaving her?

He was gone, and she was desolate without him.

When she went down to breakfast the next morning she was nervous at the thought of seeing him. Perhaps today, after last night . . . She hoped fervently he would act more warmly toward her.

When she entered the hall, he was talking to her father and Sally. Her father greeted her and she waited tensely for Robert to look up from his conversation and speak to her.

He waved to her offhandedly—"Oh hello, Katherine"—and resumed his conversation with Sally, as if she were of no importance to him at all.

She quickly seated herself at the table in a stiff, high-backed chair. For a moment the trenchers of food blurred, but she managed to control her tears and remain dry-eyed through breakfast. Somehow she managed cheerful replies when someone spoke to her.

Nothing had changed. Robert was coldly distant and she was unable to approach him. The physical closeness they had shared in the night had been meaningless. Was this to be their marriage: passionate but meaningless sex in the night, and emotional rejection during the day? Such a marriage would be unendurable. She must find a way to win him back.

She had to get away to think. After breakfast she took a walk upon the moors. A stiff wind gusted up from the sea. Normally she would have thought it a beautiful morning. The leaves of the sparse trees formed green lace against a cloudless sky, and the sea showed turquoise where it licked granite cliffs. But she noticed nothing, thinking only of Robert. How could she find a way to apologize? She wandered far from the castle, and when she became aware of her surroundings again, she found herself near the deserted mines.

The wind swept and sighed across the moors. She followed a well-beaten path, which held the imprints of numerous hooves, the deep ruts of wagon wheels. She smelled the tangy scent of rotten sea vegetation and wondered where it came from.

In the sand before her, something glittered. She knelt and picked it up. An earring. It had an ornate design and was studded with flashing emeralds. Whose was it? And from where had it come? She sifted through the sand for its mate, but not finding it, she tucked the earring into her pocket.

She noticed suddenly that the hoof prints led in the direction of a deserted mine shaft. As she followed the tracks, the odor of rotten sea vegetation grew stronger and she wrinkled her nose. Suddenly she heard a gentle, steady knocking. Ghosts of dead miners tapping beneath in the mines! She screamed and ran blindly, stumbling on a sharp rock in her path and falling. When she tried to stand up, her right ankle, already swelling with pain, collapsed, and she fell, crying out.

Hoofbeats hammered on rock, and her husband's voice was a roar above the noise of his horse.

"Katherine, what in the in the name of God are you doing here?" His face was black with fury. "Have you no sense? The night I found you, you were nearly killed not far from here. Don't you know the moors are dangerous because of the wreckers?" Glaring down at her, he saw her hobble and whiten with pain, and his voice softened. "You're hurt?"

He was beside her at once, his large, brown hands gentle on her ankle as he examined it. He lifted her to the horse. "I don't think it's broken. You're lucky there. Ankles can be nasty to set. Still, you'll have to keep off it for a while. And that should make my life easier, as you'll be confined and not up to your usual mischief."

She was surprised to see him smiling with some of his former warmth. In the past he had always been especially considerate when she was injured or troubled. After his coldness his seemingly genuine concern amazed her. Her spirits lifted.

When they reached the Bodrugans' cottage, he helped her to the loft and she sat on the bed while he bathed her ankle. He handed her a cup of spiced tea and, even though she objected to its acrid taste, he insisted she drink it.

"It will ease the pain," he said, anxiously guiding the cup to her mouth. He watched with satisfaction as she drained it.

They heard a shutter groaning in the rising wind.

"Damn that infernal thing!" He left her to secure it. Without his presence to stimulate her, she grew drowsy. He had said he would put something in the tea for her pain. Leaning back against the bed, she saw something glimmer on the timbered floor. She stretched and picked it up, her eyes barely able to focus. It was an earring exactly like the one in her pocket. Her groggy mind circled crazily. What was this earring doing in Robert's room? Had he given it to Sally? Had she lost it when she'd been here?

Katherine carefully recalled everything that had happened to her that afternoon. She had been on the verge of discovering something important when she'd become frightened by that knocking sound. Robert had come and distracted her. She visualized the path of sand leading down into the mine shaft and recalled the powerful odor of dried sea life. Had she discovered the place where the wreckers hid their goods before selling them? If so, she would only have to keep watch to discover who the wreckers were. Sooner or later they would return to the mine shaft. Again she wondered uneasily what Robert had been doing so near the shaft.

She sank against the pillow and fell asleep, while in her half-opened palm, the earring glimmered. When a brown hand stealthily removed the jewel, the sleeping girl never stirred.

In a dreamlike haze she thought that Robert returned and took her in his arms, that she gave herself to him, that he possessed her. She heard his voice, indistinct and slurred, saying, "Katherine, my darling wife, I love you."

But perhaps it was nothing more than a dream. Hours passed, and the day darkened into night before she awakened. Outside, the wind screamed. The shutter was banging again. Rising, she tried to stand, but toppled drunkenly. She felt weak and confused from sleep and drugs. Her ankle throbbed, and she sank back onto the bed.

She had never felt so confused and lost. She hobbled painfully across the room and stared out the window. The Queen's Light was out! The wind was high and the new moon would not rise for many hours. It was a perfect night for wrecking. And Robert was gone, she knew not where.

It was obvious that Robert had deliberately drugged her. It was obvious, as well, that his show of concern had been a pretense, a way to more easily deceive her.

Somewhere out at sea sailors were struggling to navigate. Without The Queen's Light to guide them, they would be blown onto the reefs, easy prey for men like . . . like Robert! Oh, she couldn't, she wouldn't believe it! And her father? What was his part in all this?

She suspected that her father and Robert were in league together. Perhaps Watty, Clara, and Richard as well. Everyone she loved.

"No, I won't accept it!" she said out loud. "I won't! I must get to The Queen's Light and somehow relight it."

Her footsteps were heavy and uncertain as she crossed the loft and descended the stairs. The pain in her ankle was intense but it supported her weight. As she opened the door of the cottage, the wind caught it and threw it back against the wall. She stumbled out into the night.

The wind was at her back, and it almost drove her to the tower that housed The Queen's Light. She entered the tower and fumbled in the darkness as she struggled to gather the materials necessary to light the torch. She struck a light, and suddenly out of a blackened corner of the tower a shadow loomed from the darkness.

"Robert!"

Behind him other shadows wavered. She recognized Tummas and another man, his face crisscrossed with wrinkles. The man from the moors!

"Ah, dear wife, you are determined to cause me trouble." He seized her and handed her to Tummas.

"So you are responsible for the light going out, for the wrecks!" she cried. "And the earrings I found—the one in the loft—you robbed some corpse to get them so you could give them to Sally! You've murdered seamen so you could enrich yourself, just as once you murdered your wife! And doubtless, now that I've found you out, you'll murder me!"

Robert did not deny her accusations. Instead he said coldly, "It's a pity that a wife must grow so quickly disenchanted with her new husband."

"You joke now? When there are people out there who—"

"I haven't time to wrangle with you!" he said impatiently. To Tummas: "Take her away. You know what to do."

Tummas bound her swiftly, purposefully, as once he had bound her before. Then he slung her over his shoulder and carried her into the storm, plunging into the high winds as if they were powerless. Would Tummas murder her, she wondered, or would Robert do it later himself?

Tummas trudged downhill and she no longer felt the wind. Everything was dark and silent. They were in the mine shaft! She smelled the now familiar stench of rotting sea things. Tummas lowered her to the ground.

"Ye'll be safe enough here, mistress," Tummas said. His voice sounded hollow and echoed in the distance. "And not up to yer usual tricks."

What a cruel irony that he concerned himself with her safety when his master intended to kill her. Then he was gone, and she was alone in the blackness.

A wild terror possessed her. Surely she would go mad. She was bound, gagged, and shut in a mine shaft. She had always been terrified of the mines. She was afraid that the wreckers—or Robert—would return, or that the ghosts haunting these mines would appear before her.

The ropes cut into her wrists but she twisted and struggled until they were raw. Still it was no use. She could not loosen them. Tonight men and women would die because she had failed them. Tonight she herself would die. Then she heard a faint knocking.

She strained to hear, but the sound didn't continue. Her thoughts grew foggy from the drug Robert had given her and from terror. She was slipping into unconsciousness. Again she heard the knocking. Something moved nearby—a rat scurrying. She felt it brush against her ankle. She tried to scream, but the gag muffled her cry. She heard the scuttle of another rat.

Then the air itself became a heavy weight of crushing blackness, and she heard and thought no more.

Chapter 15

Laughter bellowed in the mine shaft. Otto kneeled over Katherine's prostrate form and removed the gag from her mouth. She blinked her eyes against the glare of the torch someone behind him held.

"Otto?"

Again he laughed. "Your own dear brother be here to save you." He sliced the ropes that bound her hands and helped her sit up. Gradually her eyes grew accustomed to the light, and she saw Otto clearly. Other men—strangers—crowded the entrance of the mine shaft.

The shaft was like a small room. Boxes and trunks were stacked neatly against one wall. Hogsheads and bales of some soft material littered the floor. Several of Otto's men began rummaging through a trunk. One of them cursed and the other struck him in the face. They were quarreling over some item in the trunk.

Otto turned from Katherine. "Break it up!" he shouted. When the men ignored him, he rose, tore the two apart, and threw them toward the entrance of the mine shaft. "You'll do as I say! Hear?"

One of the men cursed him, but when Otto moved

toward him, another said anxiously, "He don't be meaning nothing, Otto."

Otto turned his attention once more to Katherine. The pungent smell of the sea mingling with the smell of leather and horses assailed her. An inexplicable terror possessed her. She was safe because Otto had found her, yet a chill crawled slowly up her spine. A memory slipped into place and she realized that the odor she smelled had been in the shipwrecked sailor's room the night he died.

"It were lucky I found you," Otto said. "Sir Cranston, he sent us to look for a place where the wreckers might hide their goods. How did you come to be here, Lady Kate?"

"The wreckers got me and brought me here."

"The wreckers? It were lucky for you I found you," Otto said slowly. "Sir Cranston, he sent me to look for a place where the wreckers might hide their goods."

"Never mind all that. Otto, I need your help tonight to catch the wreckers. We haven't much time!"

His knife gave a savage jerk, and her ankles were free. He looked at her strangely, as if puzzled. His shaggy brows lifted quizzically.

"Eh?" he grunted.

All her usual resentment against him was gone because she desperately needed his help. "My husband did this to me," she explained quickly. "He's the leader of the wreckers. I caught him tonight putting out The Queen's Light. He is going to come here and kill me."

"You say he be at The Queen's Light? And his men?" His words came rapidly, like bursts of cannon fire.

"They're with him."

His black eyes were intense. "It would be a good night's work to surprise them. I be on my way then to the tower and you, sister, to the castle."

"No, I want to go with you."

He was already walking away from her, singling out one of the men from the unruly group to accompany her to the castle. The man objected, but at last he shuffled toward her and knelt down, motioning her to remain silent. His eyes leered from his wrinkled face. She mouthed a wordless scream. He was the man who had assaulted her on the moors, the man who only a short time ago had been with Robert. He tried to cover her lips with his hands, but at last she managed to cry for Otto.

"Otto! Otto! Otto!" When Otto returned at the sound of her high-pitched squeal, she said, "Otto, this man was with Lord Morley only a short time ago. He's double-crossing you! He's a wrecker!"

Otto hesitated only for a moment.

"Seize him!"

The wrinkled man was already at the entrance of the mine shaft. Two of Otto's men grabbed him, but one cried out in pain. The other fell to the ground—a silent heap—and the man ran out into the night.

"Damn!" Otto whirled to face Katherine. His lips were smiling but his eyes were grim. She was afraid of him. He pulled her to her feet. "There be no one to take you to the castle. You'll have to come with us before that double-crossing devil warns them."

His eyes gleamed strangely, and she shivered, remembering how she usually disliked him. It was ironic that she was helping the man she had always detested against the man she loved.

When she came out of the mine shaft, Katherine saw the incredible: in the distance the bright glow of torchlight beamed steadily from the tower that housed The Queen's Light. She scarcely heard Otto's curse. Someone had relit the torch, but who?

One of Otto's men lifted her onto the saddle of a roan stallion. A lantern dangled from a rope tied around the animal's neck. Something about the horse worried her, but she was so caught up in the events of the moment, she could not think clearly.

The driving wind seemed to lift and carry them to the tower, where Otto pulled Katherine from the horse and ordered her to stay behind. His men drew their swords and surrounded the tower. Their racing footsteps sounded hollow on the stone. They opened the door to the tower, but before they could enter, an enormous man leapt out. His sword was a curling ribbon of reflected torchlight.

"You bloody bastards!" he cried. "I've been waiting for you!"

Three of them attacked him at once. Robert's eyes flashed black fire; his muscular body moved with the lithe grace of a dancer as he grappled with his assailants. Two more of Otto's men attacked him, but all of them were as nothing against him. He was magnificent, terrifying, and invincible.

Watching the fight in breathless horror, Katherine realized suddenly that something was dreadfully wrong. Robert was alone, and the torch of The Queen's Light was aflame. What could it mean except that Robert had been guarding the light? And if he were guarding the light, he was no wrecker!

The horse! She had seen it once before—the night Otto had returned after Nessie had drowned. She had seen the animal the night of the wreck, the same night she'd seen a light moving on the cliff. Someone had tied a lantern to a horse's neck and driven him to make it look like a ship moving on the waves.

If Robert was no wrecker then Otto . . . Of course. He had come to his hideout and found her. She had been so stupid not to have seen. His rich clothes, his fine horse, the ring he'd given Mary— And all the time she had thought her father and Robert—

For a fleeting instant Katherine was wildly joyous that her darling, her beloved Robert, was not a wrecker. But her joy was short-lived as she realized his grave danger. She might be responsible for his death!

He fought against great odds—twenty men to one.

Oh, how could she have been so stupid as to have led Otto to Robert? If only she had trusted Robert. And even now, if he lived . . . Oh, dear Lord, he had to live! Even if he never loved her again, he had to live.

Nothing mattered now except saving Robert. She had to do something to save him! She had to find her father.

Otto and his men had temporarily forgotten her and she slipped away without them noticing. When she was out of the torchlight and shrouded completely in darkness, she began to run.

She heard shouts. Someone was screaming her name, but she did not stop. Heavy footsteps drew close behind her. Something brushed her arm and tore her sleeve, but she ran on like a terrified animal—unmindful of the searing pain in her ankle. Then, above the roar of the wind, she heard a man's gasp for breath. He grabbed for her and missed. He lunged and grabbed at her again, pulling her down onto the rough earth and falling heavily on top of her. Rocks ground into her body, bruising and cutting her. Holding her with one arm, he panted, grunted, and struggled clumsily to rise. He pulled her up with him.

He was breathing easily again, and he laughed like the belching of a furnace.

"Otto! You! I should have known!"

"Your knowledge be too late to save you. I were near to murdering you once before—the night you came into that sailor's room. I were there, you know, behind the curtains."

"You killed him!"

"I had to." He gripped her by the throat and ordered her back to the tower. She tried to resist, but it was no use; he half-dragged, half carried her. When they reached the tower, Robert was still successfully holding Otto's men at bay.

Otto called to him. "Lord Morley, you'll be doing as I say now, my grand lord, or your wife'll be paying the price." The fat blade of his hunting knife pricked her neck. When Robert hesitated he added, "I'll slit her throat. It be no more to me than cleaning fowl or gutting fish." He slashed the knife viciously, and Katherine screamed.

Robert's sword clattered to the stone, and his assailants seized him. Otto's gloating laughter rang out.

"Let her go, Otto! Your quarrel is with me. You're

236

a wrecker, and it's my business to stop you. She's but a woman."

"A woman who be knowing too much."

"She's your sister, your own blood."

Otto released her. "Take them to the cliff," he commanded. His men, muttering among themselves, did not immediately obey. "Take them, you bloody fools! Tie his hands or he'll overpower us yet!" After much grumbling and disorganized efforts this was at last accomplished. The men dragged Robert to the edge of the cliff. "You'll be food for the birds and fishes soon enough, for I'll run you through."

"As your men did in Penzance."

"It be a pity you must suffer the same fate twice. Had you been smart, you would've obliged us that night and died."

"I'm sorry to have inconvenienced you," Robert said easily. His voice was light, and he looked past Otto. "Once more you'll have to dirty your sword with my blood."

"You were always one to joke, but now I be done with your jokes. You've told your last—" Otto, his sword drawn, moved toward Robert.

Robert's crisp voice stopped him. "Isn't that shadow on the waves a ship—a ship about to run aground on the reef?"

Otto's men babbled with excitement and peered over the edge of the cliff, cheering. "Aye! Aye! It be a ship! A wreck!" they cried.

"If you do not seize your share, your leader will cheat you out of it," Robert said smoothly, "as he has been doing all along. Did you know that he has two hiding places for his goods? One that all of you know and one where he keeps the more valuable merchandise, that which he saves for himself."

"Liar!" Otto rushed toward Robert, but three of his own men stopped him.

"You be cheating us all along, eh? Well, it be no surprise to me."

The rest of Otto's men lost interest in their captives. They raced past them toward a path leading down to the sea. Otto shouted at the now disorganized group to regain their attention, but they never looked back. The three men who were holding Robert released him and followed the others. Otto shouted after them to no avail.

"Idiots!" Otto spat after them, but his voice was lost in the howling wind. "Your fate be the same without them," he said, lunging toward Robert. With no one to restrain him, Robert jumped nimbly out of his reach. Katherine grabbed for Otto's hand holding the sword, but he brandished it menacingly toward her.

"Katherine, stay back or he'll kill you!" Robert commanded.

Otto lunged once more at Robert, his sword ripping the fabric of Robert's sleeve and causing him to lose his footing. A boulder tumbled into the sea as he scrambled frantically to keep from falling backward.

Suddenly a sound rose above the roar of the wind. Richard and Sir Cranston loomed out of the night like two avenging angels. Behind them stood Tummas and the wrinkled man.

"Otto, throw down your sword," Sir Cranston commanded. "Your game's up."

Katherine, uncomprehending, still grabbed for Otto's sword and, terrified, Otto struck her across the face, felling her to the ground. He hit her on the head with the hilt of his sword, and ran in the same direction his men had fled.

The wrinkled man cut the ropes binding Robert's hands. "Jammez, thank God you were in time!" Robert exclaimed.

"Tummas put 'er ladyship in the mine shaft as it were the nearest place he could think of to get her out of the weather and get to the place where we were to ambush the wreckers. He didn't think they'd come to the mine shaft before they plundered a ship."

"Tonight's been a piece of fool's blundering, for sure," Robert said.

Sir Cranston cradled Katherine in his arms; his voice was anxious. "Daughter, it's all over now. You're going to be all right."

Robert knelt beside his father-in-law, his face set in grim lines as he stared down at her. "It seems, Wife," he finally said, "I vastly underestimated your determination to bring the wreckers to justice. We've all had quite a night as a result. The drug I gave you should have put two men to sleep for a day."

"Robert . . . I . . . I . . ."

"Hush, you must save your strength. Tummas, Jammez, you must take my wife to the castle."

She tried to smile, to answer him, to beg him to understand and forgive her, but she was too weak.

Tummas mounted Otto's horse, and Robert lifted her into his arms. Then he eased himself over the edge of the cliff, and she knew that he was going after Otto.

"Oh, Tummas, do you think he'll ever forgive me for all the trouble I've caused?"

"Well, mistress, you did ask me, and I mean no disrespect. All women be trouble—that be their nature —and ye seem to be a peck more trouble than most. But then again, the captain be not as other men and his tastes in all things be peculiar. Who's to know but him if ye'r the woman to suit him." When Katherine groaned at his answer, he added, "He married ye, didn't he?"

Little comforted by his words, she sank wearily against the broad thickness of his chest. All she had left was hope. She closed her eyes, her head was soon nodding against Tummas's shoulder.

When Katherine opened her eyes again she was tucked beneath two thick blankets and resting on the sofa before the fire in her bedchamber. Clara, brisk and efficient, poured two cups of steaming herbal tea and handed one to Katherine.

"Clara, what's happened? Is Robert safe?"

"Sip your tea, dear, and I'll tell you everything." Mechanically Katherine obeyed. "First of all, Robert is safe."

"I . . . I . . . must go to him and tell him . . ."

Clara placed a restraining hand gently on the girl's arm. "Now, now, dear. I don't think that would be at all wise. Perhaps when you've fully rested."

Didn't Robert want to see her? Of course he didn't. All the events of the long day came back to her: her unfortunate part in everything that had happened. She had very nearly gotten him killed. She fell back heavily onto the sofa.

"I'll explain everything," Clara said. "Your father and your husband wanted to protect you from all this. I disagreed with them, but they were determined. They thought if you were ignorant you would be safe from the wreckers. Your husband is an agent of Queen Elizabeth sent here on a mission to discover who was wrecking Her Majesty's ships. Your father met Robert in Plymouth shortly before Robert came here, and was struck so favorably by Lord Morley that he suggested a marriage between the two families. Robert Morley flatly refused, saying one unsuccessful arranged marriage was more than enough for him. Your father at last convinced him that, when he came to Cornwall on the Queen's business disguised as Stephen San Nicholas, it would do no harm to meet you."

"And when did he agree to the marriage?"

"The night he brought you back to the castle. Robert and Jammez had already been in Cornwall a month. Robert was secretly staying in the Bodrugan cottage, and was on the verge of discovering who the leader of the wreckers was when you showed up. He had found an earring at the entrance of the mine shaft, leading to his discovery of the hiding place for the wreckers' goods. The wrecker was supposed to come to the mine shaft that night to divide up the stolen merchandise. But you appeared, and the wrecker Jammez was with attacked you. Jammez had to go along with him. Robert had to save you and abandon his plans to catch the wreckers until later. When he returned, the wreckers had removed all their goods."

"I've caused him trouble from the very beginning."

"Well, I don't think he sees it that way," Clara said. "I think he loves you very much. He couldn't tell you who he was without endangering you, himself, and his entire mission. Many people knew Robert Morley had been an agent for the Queen on other missions, and the entire investigation would have been jeopardized if his true identity were revealed. That is why he worked under the San Nicholas cover for as long as he could. But in Penzance someone discovered his true identity and informed Otto, who very nearly murdered him."

Katherine's thoughts were in a torment. Robert had had excellent reasons for keeping his identity secret. He had not deceived her to make a fool out of her. Yet she had been so ready to believe the worst of him. He must despise her, especially now after what she had done tonight.

"Then later," Clara continued, "Robert was afraid that if you learned who he really was, you would turn against him because you hated the name Robert Morley and all it represented."

And he was right, she thought. Oh, why, why have I been such a fool? Aloud she said, "You have known who Robert was all along?"

"Practically from the beginning. I discovered it quite by accident. I overheard a conversation between Richard and Robert and misunderstood. I thought they were the wreckers. When I confronted Richard with what I'd heard, he told me everything."

"I know all too well how easy it is to misunderstand when you hear only part of a conversation," Katherine said. "But tonight . . ." Her voice became anxious. When she had seen Robert last he had been grim-faced and wounded and Otto and his men still alive. "What happened tonight?"

"We can't be completely sure yet, but according to Tummas, Otto will be caught tonight, or he'll never dare show his face in these parts again."

"The ship?"

"Wrecked. But the crew survived."

"Praises be—but you . . . you haven't told me everything. I know I must have played a part in botching things up. You must tell me what has happened as a result."

"Well, as I understand it, this morning Robert found you near the wreckers' hideout, so he took you to the Bodrugan cottage and drugged you. He thought the drug and your injured ankle would keep you safely out of the way.

"But they didn't. I woke up and when I saw that The Queen's Light had gone out, I struggled to the tower to relight it."

"You're a strong girl, stronger than any of us realized. When we checked on you before nightfall, you were in a deep sleep. We thought you'd be safe."

"The shutter came loose in the wind again and woke me. I went to the tower and when I saw Robert and Jammez there, I thought they were the wreckers and had put out the light."

"You must have come before Robert had a chance to relight the torch. When he heard you, he probably hid because he thought you were a wrecker."

"I was so sure of his guilt, I said horrible, unforgivable things to him. It was just that when I saw Jammez with him—as you know, he'd attacked me or pretended to—I was so certain, so certain . . ."

"Jammez was also with the men who attacked your husband in Penzance," Clara said. "Had he not been

243

there, Robert would be dead. He persuaded Robert's assailants to leave him for dead."

Katherine considered how easy it was to misunderstand and misinterpret. She had not only betrayed Robert with her doubts, she had suspected Richard, Clara, Watty, and even her father as well. She had known them all her life—they were her family—yet she had believed them wreckers.

"Jammez was going to lead Otto and his men into an ambush tonight," Clara continued. "But the plan was fouled up when Tummas put you into the mine shaft, and the wreckers returned to their hideout and discovered you. But you know the rest. You led Otto to Robert, who had relit the lamp to try to keep the ships safe at sea while your father was capturing the wreckers. He alone had to fight the wreckers while Jammez went for Sir Cranston and Richard, who were waiting to ambush Otto."

"I certainly made a mess of things and I nearly caused Robert's death in the process."

Katherine set her cup of tea on the tray. How could she have been so wrong about everything? What did Robert think of her now? But she knew the answer. She recalled the harsh outlines of his face as he had looked at her before leaving her to pursue Otto. He no longer cared anything for her.

At that moment Mary burst through the door. "My Lady Kate, oh, my Lady Kate!" Her voice was a wail of anguish. "He be dead . . . dead . . . Otto . . . dead. He were wrecking and he were sucked into The Jaws. Your husband he did try to save him."

"Is Robert all right?"

"Your husband be sound enough. Otto's gang be

scattered in all directions. Sir Cranston and Richard be helping with the survivors of the crew from the ship. Oh, my Lady Kate . . ." She forgot their social stations and threw herself into Katherine's arms. "Jesse, she were crazed with grief over Otto. She be like Daavi when his Mathaw were feared drowned in that pool. Otto were bad like you say but she were his mother and he did have his good side." The ring Mary wore flashed. "Jesse be blaming herself for his death. You see, she never told him he were not Sir Cranston's son but the legitimate son of her husband, who were dead only a short time before Otto were born. You know Otto set such store by thinking he were Sir Cranston's. He carried himself proud. He were too proud, that were his trouble. He wanted things he weren't born to have, thinking they were his right." The girl sobbed violently, her words becoming incoherent.

Clara folded Mary into her arms and led her to the door. "You must not distress yourself unduly," she said. "What's done is done. You must remember Nessie, and count yourself fortunate that you're young and still alive. You'll find another man, a better man to love."

"Otto—he were nice to me. He were!" she wailed.

"Katherine, will you be all right while I take Mary to her room?" Clara asked.

Katherine nodded. She slipped from the sofa and pulled on her turquoise velvet dressing gown. Her body ached: her ankle, her head, her stomach, but the greatest pain was in her heart. She had betrayed Robert, she had lost him.

From the darkened landing Katherine peered down

to the brilliantly lit hall buzzing with confusion. Seamen and survivors from the wrecked ship were being served food. Pallets were being prepared; blankets were being stacked beside them. Then she saw Robert, standing apart from the others. He held Sally Bodrugan in his arms, his black head bent over hers.

The sight of them together was an agony for Katherine. She sagged against the railing. It was obvious he no longer loved her. Her father looked up and saw her. He motioned for her to descend the stairs, and when she did not, he came to her.

"Daughter, you look none the worse for this night's misadventure." His breath was heavy with ale. He pointed beneath them to Clara and Richard, who were embracing passionately. "We'll hear wedding bells again and soon, I'll warrant. Daughter, you're not listening, and it's easy to see what your problem is. You'll not be happy 'til you mend your quarrel with Robert."

"He seems to care not whether he mends our quarrel or not," she said listlessly.

Sir Cranston followed her gaze and watched Robert, who was leading Sally to a chair near one of the fires. Robert looked up and saw them standing on the landing. He bent low over Sally to say something, and then strode across the hall, taking the stairs two at a time.

"You've a good night's work to be proud of, Robin," Sir Cranston said in greeting.

"Thank you, sir. But it's not wrecking I wish to discuss. I have just received word that my services are required elsewhere. I depart tomorrow." He paused for a moment, avoiding Katherine's shocked gaze.

"Sir Cranston, I request permission to leave my wife in your safe hands until I return. It would not be safe for Katherine where I am going. And besides," he hesitated—"it might be best if we lived separately for a time."

Sir Cranston frowned darkly. "Robert," he said sternly, "the differences between a man and a woman are never settled by living apart from one another."

"Sir, the differences between Katherine and me go more deeply than most. I hope you will support me in this matter."

Robert met Cranston's gaze firmly for several moments. With a sigh of resignation, the older man nodded his consent.

Robert took one of Katherine's hands in his and kissed it. "Tomorrow, Katherine, I leave Cornwall for London and an audience with the Queen. I hope, above all things, that you will be happy." His black eyes regarded her intently, as if trying to memorize her features. "Good-bye." He seemed to tear himself away.

"Daughter, you're a fool if you don't go after him," Sir Cranston said quietly.

"Oh, Father!" She threw herself into his arms, tears flooding her cheeks. "Father, he doesn't want me any longer."

"I heard what he said, yes, but I know him and I know he loves you. He married you because he loved you. Girl, don't you see what he's doing? He wants you, but he doesn't think you want him. He loves you enough to let you go. He's a man of great courage, a man who would face anything except your rejection."

"What of Sally Bodrugan? He held her in his arms. He . . ."

"Sally Bodrugan?" Sir Cranston's voice was incredulous. "She is soon to marry one of Robin's men. Tonight he was comforting her because she'd lost Otto. Now if you've any sense, you'll go after him before it's too late. This time he'll not come to you."

He left her staring fixedly into the fire.

For Katherine the night was long and sleepless. She had been wrong about everything. Perhaps she was again wrong to let Robert go. Her father had said all along that Robert Morley was the man for her, and he had been right. When she thought of losing Robert now when she knew he was the only man for her— Oh, it would be agony! How would she stand the long years without him?

Fire turned into ashes, and the horizon was a strip of gold widening and brightening the gray sky when she left the castle. She walked slowly at first, then ran, her steps light, her ankle almost free from pain. She raced across the moors toward the Bodrugan cottage.

She almost laughed when the cottage—forlorn and lonely—came into view at last. The vast expanse of moorland stretched to the marshes on one side and the sea shone brightly on the other.

"Robert . . . Robert . . ." She burst into the cottage. After the brilliance of the sunlight outside, she squinted in the dark. "Robert!" she called. She climbed to the loft but the room was empty. All of his belongings were gone. She stared at the bed, the bed they had shared, remembering the good times they had had. But now he was gone. Surely she would never be happy again.

On leaden legs she stumbled outside, sank onto the ground, and wept. She had felt like this only once before—the day her mother died. Now there would be an empty place in her heart for Robert—an emptiness that could never be filled.

Light darkened into shadow, and she looked up. An enormous man stood between her and the sun, holding a tall beaver hat——the very latest fashion— in one hand.

"Robert, you've come back."

"You needn't worry. I've only come after my hat. You know how important fashion is to me." He placed the hat on his head and gave it a pat. "And now that I've found it, I won't trouble you further."

The hat spiraled above him like the steeple of a church. She wanted to tell him how ridiculous he looked in it, but he was leaving her and she had to stop him.

"Robert, Robert, don't go without me, please. I want to be with you always."

"What?" He gripped her fiercely and pulled her to her feet. He lifted her chin and turned her face to his, staring deeply into her eyes. "Katherine . . . darling . . ." His voice broke. "Can it be that you love me as I love you?" She nodded. "The only reason I was going was because I thought that's what you wanted."

"But I want you. I do."

Tenderly he stroked the yellow bruise on her face where Otto had struck her with his sword.

"If my hands hadn't been tied, I would have killed the lout for that."

"It was my fault," she said. "It was I who very nearly got you killed."

"None of that matters now. Do you know that when I first found you on the moors, I thought you the most beautiful woman in the world? And when I discovered who you were—that you were the woman my family wanted me to marry—I couldn't believe my good fortune. But you were so stubbornly set against me. At first I didn't tell you who I really was in order to protect you from the wreckers. Later, I couldn't bear to tell you who I was. Can you understand?"

"Oh, yes, yes. Robert, do you really love me—just me?"

"Only you—for the rest of our lives."

"There are two things I must know, then. Why didn't you make love to me that day on the cliff? Didn't you want me?"

"Of course I wanted you, my darling," he said, laughing. "But we weren't married. And strange as it seems, I wanted marriage with you first. I wanted everything set right between us before we . . . you were to be my wife, and I wanted to treat you with respect. What is your second question?" he asked with a gleam in his eye.

"Who is . . . is Lady Constance?"

He laughed. "Are you jealous?"

"Very."

"She is my aunt—quite old—a favorite relation of mine, the only person who stood by me when my father threw me out."

"Oh . . . and Sally?"

"Katherine, you said two questions, not a battery. Don't you know yet that you are the only woman for me?"

"Oh, Robert, I've been such a fool."

"No more than I. That night in the garden when I was violent, I don't know what I might have done had you not spoken, and had I not realized what you'd overheard and why you'd grown angry with me. I saw you with Blake that night and I thought—I was insane with jealously. You see, Monica, my first wife, was unfaithful to me. Our families had arranged that marriage and she, like you, had no liking for the idea. She was in love with someone else, and after our marriage, she took him as her lover. When I saw you with Blake, I thought you were like Monica. But Katherine, I didn't kill Monica, in spite of what she'd done. We quarreled on the landing, and she fell. It was an accident."

"I do believe you. Everything that has gone wrong has been my fault, not yours. I was stubborn, willful, childlike, set against a man I knew nothing about. I prejudged you. You've been so good to me—when I was hurt you took care of me. Even when I turned against you, you were always there to save me from my foolishness."

"And so, Wife, you see the error of your ways?" He was smiling broadly.

Meekly she answered, "Yes."

"It's about time, for you've sorely tried my patience."

"I'm sorry."

"We'll have to think of a way for you to make it up to me."

"I think I know a way."

His eyes on her lips lit eagerly with understanding. "Your intelligence, Wife, is your greatest asset." He bent his lips to hers. When he withdrew them, she trembled with passion. "Ah . . ." He smiled. "Not your greatest asset." He lifted her into his arms and carried her inside the cottage. "And now we must make up for all the time we've wasted, my dear wife."

"Oh, Robert."

"Robin, love," he corrected gently.

He released her and pulled something from his pocket—a simple band of gold. "The first night I brought you here, you wore this ring. Will you wear it now and for always?"

"Robin . . ." Her voice was a husky whisper.

"And now at last we'll put that bed to proper use."

"But Robin, do you intend to wear that ridiculous hat while we do?"

He held her from him then, and the cottage filled with a great burst of laughter. Reaching up to him, she silenced his laughter with her lips.

Love—the way you want it!

Candlelight Romances

INTRODUCING...

The Romance Magazine For The 1980's

Each exciting issue contains a full-length romance novel — the kind of first-love story we all dream about...

PLUS

other wonderful features such as a travelogue to the world's most romantic spots, advice about your romantic problems, a quiz to find the ideal mate for you and much, much more.

ROMANTIQUE: A complete novel of romance, plus a whole world of romantic features.

ROMANTIQUE: Wherever magazines are sold. Or write Romantique Magazine, Dept. C-1, 41 East 42nd Street, New York, N.Y. 10017